Bringing Nettie Back

Bringing
Nettie Back

Nancy Hope Wilson

MACMILLAN PUBLISHING COMPANY   NEW YORK

MAXWELL MACMILLAN CANADA   TORONTO

MAXWELL MACMILLAN INTERNATIONAL
NEW YORK   OXFORD   SINGAPORE   SYDNEY

Macmillan Publishing Company is part of the Maxwell Communication Group of Companies. Macmillan Publishing Company, 866 Third Avenue, New York, NY 10022. Maxwell Macmillan Canada, Inc., 1200 Eglinton Avenue East, Suite 200, Don Mills, Ontario M3C 3N1.

First edition
Printed in the United States of America

1   3   5   7   9   10   8   6   4   2

The text of this book is set in 11.5 point Berkeley Book.

Library of Congress Cataloging-in-Publication Data
Wilson, Nancy Hope.
  Bringing Nettie back / by Nancy Hope Wilson. — 1st ed.
    p.   cm.
  Summary: Eleven-year-old Clara's life is enriched by her friendship with the vibrant Nettie, whose family is so different from her own, but then a serious brain condition threatens to change Nettie forever.
  ISBN 0-02-793075-0
  [1. Friendship—Fiction.   2. Brain-damaged children—Fiction.   3. Mentally handicapped—Fiction.   4. Family life—Fiction.]   I. Title.
  PZ7.W69745Br   1992   [Fic]—dc20   92-7640

To my childhood best friend;
writing this has brought you back.

I am very grateful to Dr. Adelbert Ames, III, neurophysiologist; Dr. Michael Moskowitz, neurologist and neurophysiologist; and Dr. Christopher Ogilvy, neurosurgeon—all affiliated with Massachusetts General Hospital—for explaining and reviewing medical information.

Sincere thanks, as well, to Roger Tincknell, for familiarizing me with the banjo; to my critique group for their unfailing honesty, insight, and encouragement; to Judith R. Whipple, for her invaluable suggestions; to Mary Faith Wilson, for her memories; and to Nicholas Martin Simms, for knowing, before I did, that I would write.

Part I

SUMMER 1958
Oggie's Farm

One

Clara swung the hammer one last time. Right on the mark. She wished Dad were watching. Except if Dad were watching, she would have missed.

"Is it done?" her little sister, Jubie, asked eagerly.

"Can we go in it now?" her two little brothers asked at once.

"Sure," said Clara proudly. She adjusted her glasses back on her nose and gave the little hut a rough shake. It hardly wobbled at all.

"Make room for me," she said. "I'm coming in, too!"

"Make room for Raz!" Robby shouted.

The three little ones giggled as they pushed back into the shadowy corners of their new clubhouse to clear some space for Clara. She had to fold her long skinny body into a crouch and squirm in backwards. Her freckled legs and dirty bare feet stuck out awkwardly into the sunshine.

"Hey, it's nice in here," she said. "Maybe I'll keep this for *my* clubhouse."

But suddenly her sister and brothers were climbing all over her, laughing and trying to push her out the door.

"Little Kids only!" Robby shouted, and Donny and Jubie took up the chant: "Little Kids only! Little Kids only!"

There were six children in the Nelson family, with an age gap in the middle. Sometimes, for simplicity, people just called them Big Kids and Little Kids. Clara was eleven—officially a Big Kid. But especially in the summer, especially here on her grandmother's farm, Clara spent her time with the Little Kids.

Robby was only six; Donny was five; little Jubie would turn four soon. Clara made secret miniature villages with them on mossy rocks in the woods. She put on dress-up plays with them in Oggie's attic full of trunks. She played Oggie's banjo and sang songs with them. She built them this new clubhouse.

Clara ducked her head out of the hut's doorway and pretended the Little Kids had really pushed her out. She rolled away, flailing her arms and legs dramatically.

She called back in a deep, scolding voice, "You Little Kids better straighten up and fly right." She sounded just like Dad.

Jubie stuck her dark, curly head out of the hut and yelled defiantly, "No! I won't! So there!" She tumbled back into the shadows as all three Little Kids dissolved into helpless giggles.

Clara lay sprawled in the sun. Her unruly hair straggled across her face, glinting gold and orange. (One theory about her nickname, Raz, was that she was a "raspberry blonde.") She brushed the hair aside, took off her glasses, and closed her eyes.

Clara loved summer. She loved Oggie's farm. Mom had grown up here. In fact, Oggie'd grown up here, too. It wasn't really a farm anymore; Oggie just pastured someone else's heifers so that the fields wouldn't go all to brush. When Mom and the six kids and the family's four Irish setters showed up for the summer, Oggie would hobble out of her kitchen, hands on arthritic hips, and settle into a wicker armchair on the screen porch.

"Off duty for the season," she'd say.

Her three cats would settle on and around her, and she'd sit like a queen on her throne, with her deck of cards, her crossword puzzles, and a flyswatter. Sunlight would filter through the maple tree just outside and make her crown of silver hair gleam. Oggie's fingers had gone all knobby at the knuckles, so she couldn't play her banjo anymore, but she kept it leaning against the wicker chair, handy for Clara's next lesson.

Dad still had to work—at an insurance office in the city—so he stayed in Newingham, the suburban town the Nelsons called home. But Oggie's farm felt more like home to Clara. When Dad came up on the weekends, he seemed to bring Newingham with him, like some sour smell that billowed out from his car when he parked it by Oggie's barn and opened the door. Suddenly Clara would feel pinched again, unsure of herself, as she always did in Newingham.

Thinking about her father made Clara restless. She put her glasses back on, scrambled to her feet, and bent to poke her head through the door of the Little Kids' hut.

"What you need in here is some food," she said. "Let's go pick some raspberries." (Another story about her nickname was that, when she was only three, she'd gone out by herself and picked a whole pint of raspberries.)

But now Clara heard the echoey clatter of a car coming along the dirt road, down the big hill onto the flat below the house. The Little Kids raced on toward the raspberry patch as Clara stood still to listen. She heard the car stop, a silence, then the mailbox door slam shut before the car drove off again. She took off in a lanky run down the driveway, her feet already toughened against the stones. Four dogs jumped up from their sleep to bound after her down the hill.

"Raz!" she heard the Little Kids call.

"Mail!" she yelled back.

There was a letter for her. She tore it open and read it quickly, then ran back up the driveway and across the yard. She slammed through the screen porch without even acknowledging Oggie in the wicker chair. She was holding in her disappointment till she could spill it to her mother in the kitchen: "Sue can't come, either."

It was Clara's turn to invite a friend from Newingham for a week. But now even this second friend had other plans.

"Oh, Raz," Mom said sympathetically. She was standing at the kitchen table in old Bermuda shorts and an unironed blouse, leaning over to cut up the green beans that Clara had picked that morning. Mom was tan and strong and active, and her dark hair fell in untidy curls around her face. She rarely bothered to sit down to work—there'd be some reason to jump up a minute later.

Clara took a bean from the colander and ate it raw.

"This doesn't have to be the end of the world, you know," her mother said. "You can invite someone else."

"No one else likes me," Clara complained.

"Oh," said Mom. "Maybe it *is* the end of the world."

"Come on, Mom! What should I do?"

"Get a knife, pull up a chair, and help me with these beans."

"Why can't Teddy or Laura help for a change?" The other Big Kids never seemed to be around when there was work to be done.

"Because *you're* here, your brother's probably buried in a book, your sister's probably hiding so I won't see she's wearing lipstick, and *you're* the one whose world just ended."

Clara grabbed a paring knife from the dish drainer and plopped down in a chair across from her mother. Mom cut one bean at a time, but Clara liked to lop off all the stems and pointy ends of the beans first, then cut up a whole bunch at once. The Little Kids ran by outside, shouting at each other as they raced to the outhouse. There was running water at Oggie's farm, but the little spring up the hill sometimes ran dry in the summer, so only Oggie got to use the inside bathroom.

"There must be someone else you played with last year," Clara's mother began again.

In her mind, Clara scanned her fifth-grade classroom, ignoring all the boys and skipping over the popular girls, whose clique had excluded her. Then her imagining eyes came to rest on Patty Knapp. Patty had sat a few rows back, over near the windows. Clara had noticed the wide, brown eyes and the long, thick braid. Patty seemed nice, but kind of quiet and shy. Clara had thought about getting to know her, but in Newingham, Clara was kind of quiet and shy, too. And anyway, Clara'd had that ruptured appendix and been out so long that she hadn't made any new friends in fifth grade.

"Maybe I'll invite Patty Knapp," Clara said, twirling a bean by its stem.

"Patty Knapp?"

"She played with her sister a lot. They're twins."

"Oh, I bet I know Mrs. Knapp from PTA. A proper, gentle lady. Pretty Southern accent."

"Patty doesn't have an accent."

"Maybe her father's the New Englander. He's a professor, I think—at the university."

"Weird."

"Weird? Being a professor?"

"No, I mean, Patty doesn't act that much smarter than me."

"Oh, Raz. When are you gonna catch on that you're

real smart yourself—*and* pretty, and altogether quite wonderful?"

Clara took a deep breath. "Dad sure doesn't think so."

There was a silence. All Clara could hear was Mom's knife slicing a bean, then the clink of her wedding ring on the enamel colander as she picked up the next bean.

"Your father loves you, Clara—you know that," Mom said.

Loves me! Clara thought. *Are you kidding?* But by now she knew better than to argue about Dad. Mom would explain again what a rough life he'd had. The list of hardships just made Clara feel guilty and annoyed. It wasn't *her* fault Dad's mother had died when he was little. It wasn't *her* fault his father and older brother had raised him to work hard and be tough. Dad had actually gotten a scholarship to Harvard College, but as soon as he'd graduated and started a family, he'd had to go to war. The way Mom put it was that the war "just took the wind right out of his sails." And now all Dad's college friends were doctors and lawyers who owned yachts and sent their kids to fancy private schools. Somehow his own family just didn't measure up.

Clara drew the knife across her little pile of beans. To her and the other kids, Mom always defended Dad. But Clara had heard enough loud arguments to know that to Dad, Mom fiercely defended the children. "They're *children*, Alan," Mom would say. "They're *supposed* to have fun!" Her voice would get louder and louder. "They're *supposed* to have feelings; they're *supposed* to make messes and mistakes sometimes! I know *you* never had a childhood, but don't expect me to deprive them of theirs!"

Now Clara looked closely at Mom's face. Her lips were drawn tight, and her eyes focused angrily on her work. Clara wished she hadn't mentioned Dad.

"Patty's sort of shy," Clara said, steering back to safety.

Mom sighed, and her face relaxed. "What's her sister's name?"

"Nettie."

"Nettie. *That* sure sounds Southern. Maybe you should invite them both."

"Both at once?"

"You said they like to play with each other."

"What if they *only* like to play with each other?"

Knife and bean still in hand, Mom leaned forward with her knuckles on the table and looked straight at Clara. "Clara Sperry Nelson," she said. (That was another theory about the nickname—that *Clara Sperry* had become *Claraspberry*.) "Clara Sperry Nelson, if you're such a sorry specimen that no one will play with you unless there's no one else around, then no matter who comes, you'll have to find out a way to hide Laura. And Teddy. And the Little Kids, for that matter."

Clara looked down at her beans, then smiled back at her mother.

"And you and Oggie, too," she said.

"And Blue and Wade and Handy and Witch," added Mom, naming the four dogs.

16

Clara giggled. "And Winkle and Nugget and Muddle," she said, listing Oggie's cats.

Mom started on the cows. "Don't forget Buttercup and Daisy and . . . what did you name all those ladies?"

"Guinevere, and Cud, and—"

Mom interrupted. "How about you just pretend you're wonderful, and invite Patty Knapp *and* her sister Nettie."

"Anything you say, Mom." Clara pushed back her chair. "Is that enough beans?" She headed for the back door. "I said I'd help the Little Kids pick some raspberries for their clubhouse."

"Clubhouse?"

"Well, kind of a little hut I made."

"Dad would be plenty proud of that!"

"Yeah," said Clara, "except I probably forgot to put away the hammer." And she let the screen door slam.

Two

A few Fridays later, Clara was actually eager for Dad to arrive from Newingham for the weekend. She stood on the screen porch and listened for his car on the hill. She and the twins had exchanged letters, and Mom had talked to their parents—it seemed like a hundred times. Now it was mid-August. Now, with summer almost over, these "friends" she didn't even know were coming to Oggie's farm. It was weird. What if she didn't like them? What if they hated her?

"Play me a song," urged Oggie from her wicker chair. "They'll get here faster that way." She shifted stiffly, making the chair groan in sympathy with her arthritic joints. Then she added, "Just one song."

Clara turned to see her grandmother's grin. Oggie was always asking her to play "just one song"—and then "just one more."

"I want to hear the car," Clara said. She leaned her forehead on the screen. Her glasses pressed annoyingly against her face, but she stayed there, looking out beyond the lawn to the brushy field and the pond. Mist was beginning to rise from the warm pond water into the cooling evening. Clara could hear the Little Kids running around upstairs as Mom coaxed them toward bed. But no car on the hill.

Mom had made it clear that the twins could go home after just the weekend if things didn't work out. Clara took a deep breath full of the prickly, metallic smell of the screen. When she let it out, her own long sigh surprised her.

"Just one song," said Oggie again. "It'll bring them like magic. How about 'This Little Light'?"

Clara sat down and picked up the banjo. By now she could strum the chords to lots of songs, so Oggie was teaching her some "frailing," a combination of strumming and finger-picking that brought back memories of when Oggie used to play.

"Thumb on the fifth string . . . brush. . . . Right!" Oggie coached, and soon Clara could hear the tune emerging miraculously from under her fingers.

Oggie tapped her foot softly as encouragement. When the song was finished, she folded her hands across her waist and smiled with pleasure. "You play beautifully, Raz. Maybe a little timid, but if you get much better, I might have to give you that old banjo for your own."

Clara rested the banjo across her lap and tried to imagine owning such a treasure. There were glossy mother-of-pearl flowers inlaid all along the neck.

"Just one more?" Oggie suggested hopefully, but then Clara heard a car on the hill. She leaned the banjo carefully against Oggie's chair, then waited for the rumble of the wooden bridge at the bottom of the driveway to be sure that the car had really turned in toward the farm. She burst out through the screen door as the four dogs emerged barking and wagging from the garage.

Clara stopped short in the middle of the lawn. Her barefoot toes caught in the overgrown grass, and she remembered suddenly that it was her week to mow the lawn. It was supposed to be done before the weekend. She felt a silly urge to hide before Dad saw her, but there was the car.

Both twins were on her side, one in front, one in back. Clara saw only their eyes: four huge, wide eyes staring in awe at the old country farmhouse that stretched out behind her. She waved clumsily, wondering if the twins had even noticed her.

Mom came out as Dad parked the car, three doors opened at once, and everyone stood around in awkward hesitation. The twins looked exactly alike—deep, brown eyes; thick, brown hair in single braids down their backs. They were no taller than Clara's stocky father, and Clara felt suddenly spindly and gawky—she was already as tall as her mother.

As the dogs sniffed and investigated, Dad chuckled.

"I'd introduce you," he said to Mom, winking at Clara, "but I'm still not sure which is which. Let me see . . . " He held out his hand toward one twin. "This is Patty," he said decisively, but then that twin giggled—a rich, warm giggle that made her eyes sparkle.

"I'm Nettie," she said. "Hi, Mrs. Nelson." She stretched her hand toward Clara's mother, then acknowledged Clara with a broad smile.

Now Clara recognized the other twin's look of shy amusement.

"Hi, Patty," Clara said, "this is my Mom."

As Mom welcomed the twins, Dad stretched and looked around, breathing deeply, as if thirsty for country air. He was still in his business suit, and it seemed to cramp and choke him.

"Good week, Ann?" he asked Mom.

"*Great* week," Mom answered. She handed him the twin suitcases from the trunk of his car.

"No one mowed the lawn," he said, annoyed.

Clara winced.

"Oh, Alan," Mom said lightly.

They were all trailing toward the house. Nettie stopped and turned to look around. "This place is *beautiful!*"

But Clara heard Dad mutter up ahead to Mom, "Looks like a damn jungle!"

"Come meet my grandmother," urged Clara. She wanted to get the twins away from Dad.

By now, Teddy and Laura were on the screen porch, starting a card game with Oggie. They just mumbled hello, with curious eyes, but Oggie put down her cards, creaking in her wicker chair to extend her arm and shake each twin's hand.

"Call me Oggie," she said, "Everyone does. Even my son-in-law. Even the milkman. Have you had anything to eat?"

As Nettie described the feast of homemade fried chicken that Mrs. Knapp had packed for the car ride, Clara could hear Mom and Dad in the kitchen—Dad all annoyed, Mom all defensive. Clara wished she'd remembered to mow the lawn.

"Mama sent some of her pies," Nettie was adding. "And a few loaves of bread."

The sounds from the kitchen were getting louder.

"Come see my room," Clara said impatiently.

As she led the twins up the front stairs, she heard Mom go up the back ones.

It was getting dark, and the flowered wallpaper in Clara's room seemed dim. She flicked on the light. Patty sat down on the cot Clara had set up at the foot of the twin beds. Nettie plopped down beside her sister and looked around.

"This is neat," she said, smiling at Clara.

Four huge eyes faced Clara again, two that seemed to watch her carefully, two that seemed to dance with expectation. Now Dad had come upstairs, and his voice droned on from the room down the hall. Mom had gone silent.

"Want to go skinny-dipping?" Clara said suddenly. The four wide eyes grew still wider. Clara sucked in her breath, as if the words might be drawn back in and swallowed.

She had forgotten. Here on the farm, she got so comfortable, so used to Oggie's open approval. Even Mom seemed to relax about everything until Dad showed up for the weekend. From Monday to Friday, it didn't matter if Clara's hair was a nest of snarls. It didn't matter what clothes she put on or when she got around to making her bed. She got so used to the way her days spread out over the land without any shape or edges, that she did stupid things like forgetting to mow the lawn. Like asking new friends to go skinny-dipping. She'd never dare mention such a thing in Newingham. Maybe the twins would be shocked. Maybe they couldn't even swim.

"Skinny-dipping? Sure!" said Nettie, as Clara let her breath out again. "Where?"

Dad had gone downstairs and Mom was folding laundry when Clara passed her parents' room in search of towels.

"We're going skinny-dipping, Mom."

"Okay, honey. Mrs. Knapp says they're good swimmers. But not over your head at night, remember."

"I know."

"And Clara . . . "

"What?"

"Guests or no guests, you'll have to find time to mow the lawn tomorrow."

Carrying the biggest towels Clara could find, the three girls headed down the stony driveway in the gathering darkness.

"Don't your feet hurt?" Patty asked Clara. The twins were wearing sandals, but Clara was barefoot, as always.

"They're like leather by now," Clara answered. She laughed a little to hide her sense of pride.

"Better start training mine!" Nettie said. She gripped Clara's shoulder with one hand as she leaned over to pull off her sandals.

"Ouch!" she squawked with the next step, and giggled that wonderful giggle. "Ouch again!" Her big towel and her dangling sandals swung wildly as she jerked her arms with each step. She looked like a flapping, drunken marionette, and Clara imitated her all the way down the driveway, till all three girls were lost in laughter.

At the wooden bridge, Nettie stopped and pointed down the brook to the pond. "Look!" The mist was now a glowing column, rising higher and higher, as if stretching to catch the last lingering light. "It's beautiful," she said quietly.

Then, abruptly, she sat down in the road and addressed her bare feet. "Had enough for the first day?" She paused as if listening to an answer, then replied in mock annoyance. "Okay, okay—you don't have to yell!" And she put her sandals back on.

When they reached the pond, Clara slipped right out of her clothes and laid her glasses on top of the pile. She was suddenly glad for the darkness that hid her big, ugly appendix scar, and she wondered what else she'd forgotten to worry about.

"Have to stay near the dam," she said, wading in.

When a hot summer day had faded into a cool evening, the pond water was so much warmer than the air that it felt thick, velvety, an entirely different substance from the sharp crispness of an afternoon swim. Clara had experienced this all her life, yet it surprised her still. She envied the twins feeling it for the first time, and laughed at their gasps of pure amazement as first Nettie, then Patty followed her into the water.

"This is neat!" crowed Nettie.

Both twins had pinned their long braids up on their heads, and they looked like twin beavers, gliding along with their chins jutting out.

By the time the three girls picked their way up the little path back to the road, the night had truly come. The lights of the house, which had seemed so bright across the pond, were now almost hidden by towering spruces. From long practice, Clara could discern the smoother, paler darkness that indicated the hard-packed dirt stretching in front of them, so she took a slight lead as they shivered and chattered back to the house.

Clara lay on the cot that night looking into the darkness that hid the ceiling. Nettie had made them all giggle for awhile, and then she'd suddenly gone to sleep. Now at last, even Patty's breathing sounded deep and steady. Clara wondered if they would stay beyond the weekend.

Then she realized with surprise that she already hoped they would.

Three

A t breakfast the next morning, there were eleven in the tottery chairs around Oggie's old dining-room table. Mom had made a big pot of oatmeal, and the milk carton and sugar bowl were on the table among the scattered bowls and spoons. Clara's older brother, Teddy, circled the table with the oatmeal pot, serving a big sloppy spoonful over each person's shoulder. The Little Kids fussed and giggled.

Dad had come to the table in old cut-off dungaree shorts, work boots, and a clean white undershirt that Clara knew he would shed the minute he got out into the sun. "Oggie," he said, "How about I cut away some of those alders from around the springhouse? They're drinking all your water."

Oggie smiled affectionately at Dad. "Thanks, Alan. I don't know what I'd do without you."

This was one of Oggie's favorite lines, and Clara had to admit that without Dad's constant mowing and scything and bringing in firewood, Oggie probably would have sold the farm years ago.

"But you know, Alan," Oggie went on, "You could *relax* for a minute, too!"

Dad looked at Mom. "Too much of that going on already," he said.

"Please pass the sugar," Clara said quickly.

"You just had it," Laura said.

"Well *I* need some," piped up little Jubie.

Clara kept talking. "You Little Kids want to ride the cows today?"

Patty looked up to see if Clara was joking. Nettie laughed as Robby and Donny and Jubie all shouted at once. "Yeah!" "Can we, Mom?" "I hosey I go first!" (*Hosey* was the Little Kids' favorite word these days—whoever said it first was supposed to claim unquestioned rights to some privilege.)

Little Jubie turned to Nettie. "Want to come? It's fun!"

"Clara," Mom asked pointedly, "is there plenty of gas for the lawn mower?"

Nettie looked with surprise at Clara. "You mean you get to use the *power* kind? Can I help?"

Dad smiled at her. "That's the spirit, Patty!"

Nettie smiled brilliantly back. "I'm Nettie."

"Nettie," Dad repeated, and chuckled.

Jubie looked sulky.

"Don't worry, Jube," said Clara. "First the lawn, *then* the cows, okay?"

"We'll get the apples!" Jubie burst out. She jumped up, and her chair tipped over.

"Sit still, Julia!" Dad said.

"Alan, for heaven's sake, she's only four!" said Mom, helping Jubie back into her chair.

Then two of the dogs came wagging in from the garage and had to be let out again. Jubie insisted on pouring her milk herself, and spilled. "Why'd you let her pour?" Dad complained to Mom. Laura stood up to avoid getting milk in her lap, and her chair tipped over. "Laura!" Dad scolded. Nettie laughed and grabbed a bunch of paper napkins to sop up the spill. Patty sat with an uncertain smile and eyes that grew wider and wider until Teddy asked her to pass the milk.

By the time the flurry of passing and pouring and spooning out sugar had reached the last waiting person, the first to be served was sipping the last drop of milk from an empty bowl and jumping up to begin the day.

Dad went into the garage to get the big brush clippers, his scythe, and the sharpening stone. Then he disappeared up the hill toward the springhouse.

It wasn't till late afternoon that the Little Kids finally got their chance to ride the cows. They ran ahead of Clara and the twins and clambered up onto the bar-way, a pasture gate made of four stripped trees suspended across the opening like huge ladder rungs. Robby and Donny jumped down on the other side, but Jubie perched precariously at the top and waited for Clara to help her over.

They all climbed the slope to the Slippery Rock, every pocket bulging with green apples from the old tree by the outhouse. As the heifers gathered around them expectantly, Patty looked a little scared.

"I hosey I go first!" claimed Jubie. She stood on the high end of the Slippery Rock—a huge, pinkish-white rock with a surface so smooth, so flat, and so tilted, that generations of children had used it as a slide.

Clara lifted Jubie onto Buttercup's patient brown back, and Nettie held out an apple. Buttercup followed Nettie, making Jubie squeal with delight. Clara lifted Donny onto Daisy, then boosted Robby up onto Cud. Patty watched from the Slippery Rock as cows lumbered after apples and children slid about, screaming, on the cows' backs. Nettie laughed and laughed. "This is neat," she said, and threw her arms around Buttercup's broad neck in an enthusiastic hug.

That night, when the Little Kids were in bed and Oggie was playing cards with Laura and Teddy and Patty, Clara played the banjo and watched Nettie draw. Now Clara remembered that Patty had once referred proudly to Nettie as "a born artist," but nothing had prepared Clara for this magic: Just a few broad strokes with a stubby pencil, and suddenly, incredibly, there on some old sheet of notebook paper was curly-headed Jubie, clinging gleefully to Buttercup's neck. On the back of that page, Nettie drew herself, apple in outstretched hand. She giggled richly as she added a wild, flying braid and huge, comical big toes. Then she went on to the next page.

By Sunday evening, Clara was pretty sure Nettie would want to stay all week at Oggie's farm. But Patty had mostly read and played cards all weekend.

"I thought Patty would make you leave," Clara confessed to Nettie.

They'd all three been up by the Slippery Rock picking flowers when Dad had left for Newingham. Then the Little Kids had called Patty in to read them their bedtime story again.

Clara and Nettie sat on the smooth rock watching the mist rise off the pond.

"Are you kidding?" said Nettie. "Patty really likes it here, too."

Clara took off her glasses and let the whole world go misty.

"Patty *loves* reading all the time," Nettie explained. "At home, she knits a lot, too."

"Like Teddy," Clara added.

"Teddy *knits*?"

Clara laughed. "I meant the reading." Then she laughed harder. "I can just see it—Teddy knitting! Dad would *really* have a fit!"

"Your dad was real nice on the way up here—told us war stories—those plane crashes and all."

"Plane crashes?" Clara put her glasses on and tried to focus.

"Amazing," Nettie added. "Almost dying like that—*twice*."

Clara stood up impatiently. Dad had finally left, and now Nettie was keeping him here. Clara whacked idly at some tall grass as she started down the hill toward the bar-way and the house. Dad had never told *her* about any plane crashes. She turned and walked backward a few steps as Nettie caught up.

"Mom says *I* almost died last year," Clara ventured. "My appendix ruptured."

"Scary," Nettie said respectfully. "I never even get sick."

"I don't really remember the worst night—just being in the hospital and calling the nurses and then lots of weird dreams." Weird dreams Clara could still see vividly, but had never described to anyone—dreams of Jubie in a yellow dress, dancing in airy circles and waving good-bye; dreams of Dad sitting by the bed crying and crying. Ha! Dad wouldn't even cry if she *did* die! And anyway, the hospital didn't allow kids to visit, and Jubie'd never had a yellow dress.

"Watch your head," Clara said as Nettie ducked through the bar-way after her.

They didn't talk about Dad again all week long. Patty still stayed on the porch a lot—she read alone or to the Little Kids and played cards with Oggie and Laura.

Clara and Nettie climbed to the high, high platform in the barn and called in spooky voices through the dimness to the Little Kids, giggling below. They tore out the beaver dam up the brook, spattering themselves so thickly with mud that they ran for soap and towels and walked the half-mile to the "summer bathtub"—a little swimming hole hidden in the woods. There, in just their underwear, they slid down the slimy moss bed of the waterfall, landing with shrieks in the cold pool below. On a rainy day, Nettie organized a play with the Little Kids. Even Patty joined them this time, as they dressed up in the top hats and ostrich plumes and whale-boned dresses from the trunks in Oggie's hot attic.

Mom kept taking Clara aside and reminding her to include Patty more.

"It's not my fault," Clara finally protested. "We keep asking, and she keeps saying no."

"You and Nettie have hit it off so, maybe she doesn't feel welcome."

"Come on, Mom! She just likes different stuff! Sometimes she *knits* all the time, Nettie says."

"Don't be mean, Raz. You knit sometimes, too. Patty's a very sweet girl."

"Come *on*, Mom! I didn't say she wasn't. I *like* Patty, but. . . . " Clara's own thought surprised her. She'd been about to say Nettie was her best friend. Weird. She'd only met Nettie a few days ago.

And soon Dad would be coming back and taking Nettie away again.

Mom interrupted Clara's thoughts. "I know what you

mean, Raz," she said. "Patty does seem fine. And Oggie's talked to her a lot. I guess the Knapp household's *very* different from ours."

Clara was so busy marveling at the meaning of *best friend*, she didn't think to question the meaning of *very different*.

Four

That next Friday, Nettie passed all Mom's safety tests so that she could mow the lawn herself. While Clara and Patty helped the Little Kids decorate their clubhouse with some of Nettie's drawings, Nettie pushed the roaring mower back and forth, singing at the top of her lungs.

Dad arrived late that night, so Clara didn't know if he noticed the lawn.

"Oggie," he said as everyone was finishing Saturday breakfast, "I want to bring in some of those dead maples from the old sugar lot. Great splitting wood."

"Thanks, Alan. Believe me, I think of you warmly all winter long." Oggie grinned a little at the double meaning in her words, then added, "I don't know what I'd do without you."

"Teddy," said Dad, calling him back from the bottom of the stairs, "I'll need some help with the wood."

Clara noticed Laura slip out the garage door. Laura always managed to hide until it was safe to come back and play cards with Oggie.

Teddy turned toward Dad with a stubborn look. "Mom said I could go into town with her." To Teddy, *town* meant the library.

Dad glanced at Mom, who gave the slightest nod back. Clara didn't want the twins to hear Dad's lecture about "noses in books on a fine summer day," or maybe it would be the one about "learning to do a little real work," or "taking a little responsibility around here."

"Can I drive the tractor?" Clara asked quickly. She ate her last bite of egg and stood up carefully so that her chair wouldn't tip over.

"Sure," said Dad, with only a quick, doubtful glance at the twins.

Clara had to put on shoes to drive the tractor, but it was worth it. She inched out of the barn in first gear, only jerking a little as she let the clutch bar up.

"Good," coached Dad. "Now stand on 'em both!"

The old tractor had to stop to shift gears, and to stop, the driver had to press down the clutch bar with one foot, the brake bar with the other. Clara could only do that by standing with her full weight astraddle. The tractor stopped abruptly. Clara rattled the big upright shift lever into neutral.

"Now neutral!" called Dad over the noisy engine. He was loading his chain saw and gear into the rickety open trailer.

"I already did," shouted Clara, still standing on the brake bar, but twisting to watch him. He signaled her with one thumb up, and grinned. Nettie was hovering eagerly near him.

"Up here, Patty—it's safer to sit up front," he said.

Nettie laughed. "I'm Nettie."

"Really? I thought I had it right this time."

Clara couldn't believe anyone would mistake Nettie for Patty.

The huge rear wheels of the tractor had curving metal fenders that spread out behind the driver's seat like a pair of wings. Dad showed Nettie how he sat braced against one fender, and Nettie took her place opposite him. She and Clara waved to Patty, who'd decided to go into town with Mom and Teddy and the Little Kids.

"Can I do third?" asked Clara. In third gear, and with no load in the trailer, the tractor would actually go fast enough to create a little wind in her hair.

"Okay," said Dad, "but let 'er up easy."

As the tractor bumped and bounced down the driveway and across the wooden bridge, Clara lifted her face into the wind and felt happy. She could sense Dad's watchful, critical presence over one shoulder, but over the other poured Nettie's exuberance.

"This is neat!" crowed Nettie, and Dad chuckled.

Clara stood up to stop the tractor and shift into second for the slow trip up the old logging road into the woods. She was just settling back and thinking of singing when Dad said sharply, "Don't ride the clutch!" Clara always forgot to take her foot off the clutch bar after she shifted. She tightened her grip on the steering wheel and paid closer attention all the way to the first felled tree, where Dad took over to back the trailer into place.

Dad cut up the tree while the girls loaded the stove-length pieces into the trailer and made a pile of the branches that were too small to use. It was satisfying work. Clara loved the mixture of smells: the sweet sawdust, the oily sharp smell of the chain saw, the rising dampness of the ferns crushed underfoot.

Nettie's face was flushed as she helped Clara lift a big section of tree trunk. Together they heaved their burden into the back of the trailer. Nettie brushed the bits of bark off her hands and took a deep breath. "It all smells so good!" she exlaimed over the noise of the saw.

When the trailer was full and the saw was silent, Dad looked at Nettie and grinned. "Ready for your turn?"

Nettie was laughing as she climbed into the driver's seat, but she listened intently to Dad's instructions. Then Dad pressed the starter button and showed Nettie where to set the throttle. He climbed up onto the fender opposite Clara and winked at her.

"Hold on tight!" he warned cheerfully.

The tractor jerked madly as Nettie let out the clutch. Dad had started her in first gear, so progress was slow through the woods, but Nettie looked as eager as a race-car driver.

Then suddenly Nettie burst out, in a deep, scolding

voice, "Don't ride the clutch!" With dramatic exaggeration, she lifted her foot from the clutch bar and placed it on the footrest, talking back to herself in mock annoyance. "Okay, okay, you don't have to yell!" And she giggled that rich, warm giggle.

Clara's stomach tightened a little, but when she looked up, Dad just grinned, then winked at her again. He let Nettie shift into second after they came out of the woods and crossed the road into the driveway.

By suppertime, Dad had taken a swim and changed into fresh clothes. He came to the table looking sunburned and satisfied. Through the main part of the meal, everyone got silly because the chicken was so tough that it made their jaws ache from chewing.

"Don't laugh," said Mom, laughing. "I'll patent this— a new form of leather. We'll be rich!"

Dad chuckled. "Tough chicken'll put you all through college," he said, smiling around at his children, "so I can retire."

"And move up here," Mom added.

Dad sighed. "And really take care of this place."

As the Little Kids clamored excitedly, hoping the part about moving to Oggie's wasn't a joke, Dad winked at Oggie. "With your permission, of course."

Oggie smiled and nodded, but couldn't speak. She was busy chewing and chewing.

Clara swallowed dramatically and pretended to scold Nettie: "Take that gum out of your mouth, young lady! No gum in my classroom!"

Nettie's eyes danced as she pulled a long face. "But it's not gum, teacher," she said. "I'm still chewing last month's chicken!"

Then Robby and Donny and Jubie had to repeat the joke over and over, with lots of variations, till Mom told them to settle down and eat something if they wanted dessert.

"What's for dessert?" asked Jubie.

"Those blackberries you helped pick."

Jubie looked doubtful. She didn't have to eat tough chicken to get blackberries.

"Over ice cream," added Mom, reaching out to tickle Jubie.

Patty helped Clara clear the table, and as Laura circled to serve vanilla ice cream from a dripping cardboard carton, Dad leaned back and looked around.

"So Teddy," he said, "did you get a real workout lifting those books today?" Dad winked at the twins as if this were another joke, but Clara felt the air turn electric.

"Oh, Alan," said Mom. Teddy looked intently at his ice cream.

"Well," Dad insisted, "it wouldn't do any harm for him to take a little responsibility around here."

Mom was silent, but Clara could feel a familiar tension course between her parents. Without even exchanging glances, they seemed to focus exclusively on each other. It was as if a thunderstorm were gathering high overhead, casting an uncertain darkness on everyone else. As yet, the silent lightning flashed only from cloud to cloud, but Clara knew how suddenly it could veer toward a new target.

Dad cleared his throat. "Really, Ann, it wouldn't kill these kids to do a little real work once in a while! I mean even Patty here. . . . " He smiled, but it came out twisted and sour. Patty glanced at Nettie, looking a little frightened. Dad paused to shake some blackberries onto his ice cream and pass the rest on. "Even Patty here helped with the wood."

Nettie laughed. "I'm Nettie."

But Dad didn't seem to notice this time. Clara's skin prickled with embarrassment as Dad kept going, warming to his lecture. " . . . teach them some responsibility . . . when I was their age. . . . "

"No fair," Donny suddenly whined. "Robby took too many berries."

"They'll never get anywhere in life if they think it's all a big game."

Clara stared at her hands, one poised with her spoon, the other resting by her bowl. They still felt all rough from loading wood, and the fingertips were purple from berry picking.

"I worked a lot today, Dad," she said. She tried to sound matter-of-fact, but it came out whiny.

"Watch your tone of voice, young lady!"

"But, Dad—" she started.

"Don't talk back, Clara Nelson!"

Clara swallowed hard. The lightning had struck. Hot humiliation pressed at the back of her eyes, but she was determined not to cry.

"I just—"

"None of your guff, young lady. Your mother may put up with that stuff, but I won't."

"It's not *Mom's* fault!" Clara heard herself yell. Her muscles felt so charged, she was afraid she'd throw her ice cream at him. She stood up and headed for the garage door, hearing her chair clatter to the floor just before she slammed the door behind her. As the dogs jumped up and ran eagerly ahead of her, Dad called angrily from inside, but Clara didn't even pause till she was through the bar-way and up the hill to the Slippery Rock.

The screen door slammed a few minutes later. The dogs bounded down the hill to greet the newcomer, and Clara knew, before she looked, that it was Nettie. She came up through the pasture carrying Oggie's banjo, and sat down next to Clara without a word.

"Sometimes I really hate him," Clara said, seething.

"He was fun about the tractor," Nettie ventured.

Clara felt annoyed at her for missing the point. "That's 'cause the tractor's *his* toy. Anything *he* does is real important. If all I ever wanted to do was mow things, and cut wood, and ski, and earn money, he'd probably think I was a great kid—except for being a girl, of course."

"He doesn't act all that nice to Teddy."

Clara sighed and took the banjo from Nettie. She brought her knees up so that she could lean forward and play. "That's 'cause Teddy reads all the time." She started singing almost in a whisper, pausing to get the frailing right. " 'This little light o' mine—' "

"Like Papa."

42

"What? 'I'm gonna let it shine.' "

Nettie leaned back on her elbows and looked at the sky. "My Papa reads all the time."

" 'Oh, oh, oh,' " Clara sang timidly. She tried to remember if she'd ever seen Dad read anything but the newspaper. At home, he was always reading the newspaper. All he ever did was get up, get dressed in a suit, read the newspaper, go to work, come home, read the newspaper. Except on weekends all winter—then he *always* made *everyone* go skiing. " 'This little—' "

"I wonder if Papa's been missing me," Nettie said to the sky.

Clara stopped playing. "Do you miss them?"

"Of course."

Clara tried to imagine missing her father. Then she tried to imagine next week without Nettie. "So you're glad the week's over?"

Nettie sat up abruptly. "Are you kidding? I could stay here forever!"

"It's nice here, isn't it?"

"*Nice?* She calls this *nice?*" By now, Nettie's giggle was like a reassuring hug to Clara. "More like fantastic, I'd say! Swimming and cows and Little Kids and power things—and a best friend on top of that."

Clara's heart jumped with surprise. "So you think so, too?"

"*Think* so! Are you kidding? We're best friends, Raz. We were best friends the minute I got here."

"I know," said Clara. "It's weird."

"It's neat!" said Nettie.

"You'll have to come back," said Clara.

"Summer's almost over," Nettie said regretfully.

"I know." Clara hated leaving Oggie's. It felt like being kicked out of paradise. "And Oggie closes off most of the house after we leave."

"There's still Newingham—and school. . . . "

"It's not the same in Newingham."

"So you better invite me back next summer."

Then Clara laughed. "Next summer for sure," she vowed. She held up her hand as if taking an oath in court. "And I promise—no tough chicken."

Nettie smiled back at Clara without laughing. Then suddenly she tugged at the neck of the banjo. "Let me try that thing."

Clara handed the banjo into her friend's lap. "Want to know some chords?"

"Chords?" And Nettie started to strum loudly, just moving her left hand any old which way so that it looked like it knew what it was doing. She threw her head back and bellowed. " 'This little light o' mine, I'm gonna let it shine!' "

Clara joined in, singing at the top of her lungs. " 'Oh, oh, oh, this little light o' mine . . . ' " Nettie strummed wildly and tunelessly, and they sang the whole song through, twice over. Then Clara started a new song Oggie'd been teaching her. " 'Amazing grace,' " they wailed. Their voices seemed to fill the air around them and drift off in all directions, down the hill that way toward the misty pond, and that way toward the house. " 'Amazing grace, how sweet the sound!' "

44

Part II

FALL 1958
Newingham

Five

School had begun. This year it was Nettie in Clara's class. They both had the new teacher, Miss Ziff, and they could already tell she had a mean streak. Lucky Patty had sweet old Mr. Piper.

Clara sat on a playground swing waiting for Nettie as the other walkers ran or dawdled toward home and the buses thundered away from the parking lot on the other side of the school. She had set her books down by a post and laid her glasses on top of them.

It was Friday. This afternoon, for the first time, she'd go home with the twins, meet their parents, stay for dinner. She wished she hadn't spattered spaghetti sauce on her blouse at lunchtime. And she knew without a mirror that there were ridiculous little pointy ends sticking out all along her puny braids.

She pushed with her feet to turn the swing around and around until the twisted rope pressed against her neck and made her bow her head. Then she closed her eyes and lifted her feet, curling into a spinning ball.

"Where's Nettie?"

Clara wobbled to a stop and tried, unsuccessfully, to focus her dizzy eyes on Patty.

"Staying after."

"Again?"

"It's only the second time."

"The second time this year, and we've only had a week of school!"

"Miss Ziff was picking on Tim York again."

Clara finally felt steady enough to stand up and fetch her glasses. She sat back down on the swing.

Patty sat down on the next swing over and absently leaned back and shook her head so that her long thick braid fell down her back. She rested her arms on the books in her lap.

"What did Nettie say this time?" she asked.

"Well, you know. Miss Ziff's yelling at Tim for talking in the walkers' line, and Nettie has to pipe up about how lots of us were talking in line, so why yell at Tim? Boom! 'Take your seat, Lynette Knapp. You'll be leaving late today.' "

The door to Miss Ziff's classroom opened, and Nettie came out onto the steps, holding two blackboard erasers. She smiled broadly at Patty and Clara and leaned over the railing to clap out clouds of chalk dust. Then she turned to face her audience. She stood tall, then bowed deeply, with one arm at her waist, the other flying behind her. She giggled, then disappeared back into the classroom.

A few minutes later, she appeared again with her books. She always took books home, even though she seemed to get all A's without opening them much. Mostly she had tattered spiral notebooks full of drawings. Those she opened all the time.

Clara stood up from the swing and smoothed her skirt self-consciously. She wiggled her toes inside her saddle shoes. After Oggie's farm, it took months for her feet to get used to being cramped.

Nettie ran down the steps and headed away from the swings, toward home.

"Good-bye, Miss Ziff, have a good weekend!" she called toward the open classroom windows.

As Clara ran with Patty to catch up, she was sure she heard Miss Ziff call back cheerfully, "Good-bye, Nettie, same to you!"

"Isn't she mad at you?" Clara asked, pushing her glasses back into place.

"Nah," said Nettie. "I washed all the blackboards and watered her plants. I kind of like her."

"Weird," said Clara with amazement. "I've never stayed after except for fun."

"I haven't, either," said Patty, "but Nettie always has to say what she thinks. Some teachers hate that."

"Still," Nettie said as she gave her sister's braid a

teasing tug, "I've never stayed after except for fun." She grinned. "Race you home!"

"Should we use the Royal Copenhagen, Mama?" Patty asked.

Clara stood in the pantry between the kitchen and dining room, trying not to gape. There were four full sets of delicate china arranged behind the glass doors of the white cupboards. She had just helped Patty spread a linen tablecloth over the rosewood table, and now, apparently, came the choosing of the china.

"No, dear," called Mrs. Knapp's gently drawling voice. "Just the Spode tonight, I think."

Mrs. Knapp was in the kitchen, brushing melted *real* butter onto some fancy unbaked dinner rolls that Patty swore were homemade. Mr. Knapp was upstairs in a room they called his study. Nettie was upstairs, too—the twins were supposed to get their homework done right away on Friday nights. Patty would do hers while Nettie helped clean up after supper—or rather, after dinner. The Knapps called it *dinner*.

Patty slid back one of the cupboard doors and handed Clara a stack of five soup bowls that looked like deep plates. Clara was relieved that this set of china seemed relatively sturdy. It was still terrifyingly thin, but some of the other stuff looked like it would break if you breathed on it.

Patty counted out five big plates, five little plates, and five saucer-sized plates. She closed the cupboard carefully and pushed through the swinging door to the dining room, holding it open for Clara. Clara quickly offered to do the silverware so that she wouldn't have a chance to drop any china. Patty opened a velvet-lined drawer in the sideboard: real silver, each piece neatly nested next to the matching ones. Seeing Clara hesitate, Patty instructed her solemnly.

"Those are the salad forks, see? So they go on the outside."

Two forks and two spoons at every place, a little plate with a butter knife just above the knife and spoons, cloth napkins in silver napkin rings.

Clara's family had some real silverware, too. Oggie had given it to Mom, and it had the initials of some great-aunt on it. They used it all the time. The little forks were for the Little Kids. The Big Kids and Mom and Dad ate everything with the big forks—even salad, which they just heaped onto the plates beside the meat and potatoes. Sometimes the Little Kids used the little butter knives, but several of those had gone down the kitchen disposal with the orange peels and eggshells and coffee grounds. Mom had rescued the twisted, mangled knives and set them on the windowsill, as if she might get around to having them fixed someday.

Now Patty had disappeared through the swinging door. Clara couldn't help folding her hands as she stood waiting.

At Clara's house, there was even a pantry between the kitchen and the dining room, and a set of dishes with those wide, shallow bowls. But if the Nelsons had soup, it was their whole meal. They used the deep crockery bowls that didn't break even if you dropped them. They crumbled saltines into their soup, scattering crumbs that the dogs would later lick up from the floor.

Patty came back and handed Clara a kitchen plate full of butter pats.

"Just put a couple on each bread plate," she said. "I'll get the saltcellars and the pepper grinders." The pantry door swung after her again.

Clara surveyed the gleaming table. The smell of fresh bread was making her hungry. She gathered her concentration to be sure she'd get the butter on the right plates. Just then, Nettie appeared from the hall with some white composition paper in her hand. Miss Ziff had assigned a theme on "The Best Day of My Summer."

"What'd you write about?" Clara asked. "Do I put these on the edge or in the middle?"

Nettie's eyes danced with mischief as she took the plate of butter from Clara's hand, replacing it with the sheets of paper: "Look."

Nettie managed to watch Clara with an expectant grin even while circling the table and deftly placing two butter pats just inside the rim of each bread plate.

Nettie's "composition" was just a series of drawings: Clara pulling a branch from the beaver dam, her glasses all spattered with mud; a half-naked Nettie in a waterfall, arms and legs and braid flying. Clara glanced at the dinner table and remembered Mom saying something about the Knapp household being "very different." She tried to imagine tough chicken or big globs of oatmeal on this fancy china. She felt suddenly embarrassed.

"I don't think Miss Ziff will approve," she said to Nettie.

Nettie practically tossed the empty butter plate onto the sideboard and reached for the drawings. She smiled. "Look at this one."

Unmistakably, there was Miss Ziff. She had a stern look, and one arm stretched out commandingly. Her pointing finger was comically huge. Clara laughed. She could just hear Miss Ziff: "Take your seat, Lynette Knapp."

As Patty reappeared with two sets of salt and pepper, Mrs. Knapp called softly from the kitchen, "Dinner's ready, dear. Please tell Papa."

Patty grinned and hurried out to the hallway to yell up the stairs, "Papa! Dinner!"

Mr. Knapp was a tall, broad-shouldered man with big glasses, bushy eyebrows, and thick, brown hair. He presided at the head of the table with grand gestures and a deep, lively voice.

"Mmm!" he said, ladling out everyone's soup from a tureen that matched the plates. "Cream of cauliflower. My favorite."

Clara watched the twins closely so that she wouldn't make a mistake. She drank delicately from the side of the huge soup spoon, and when the delicious soup was almost gone, she tipped her soup plate away from her to slide her spoon under the last bit. She dabbed at her lips with the linen napkin. She had made it through the first course.

Nettie was just swallowing the last of her soup. "Yummy, Mama!" she exclaimed. Then she grabbed her soup plate, lifted the edge of the tablecloth, and ducked underneath to lick her plate clean. Mr. Knapp threw his head back and boomed with laughter. Nettie emerged licking her lips, then laughed along with her father, as Mrs. Knapp smiled patiently.

After that, Clara just watched Patty. Clara wanted to get everything right. She made no mistakes with her salad, and by the main course, she began to relax. This was fun. Like being in a fancy play. She wanted to belong here. She wanted to be part of this gleaming world with a king at the head of the table.

Mr. Knapp did lots of weird things. He talked to Mrs. Knapp about a book he'd been reading. He asked Nettie and Patty if they'd started the new books he suggested. (Patty had; Nettie hadn't.) He asked them about school. He told funny stories about when he was in school.

"Once I lost a spelling bee on the word *kidnap*," he said, grinning at Clara. "Simple enough word, right?"

Nettie giggled, and Clara smiled, waiting.

"Easy," Mr. Knapp went on, and as he spelled the word, Patty and Nettie joined in: "K-i-d-k-n-a-p-p!" And that wonderful laugh erupted again.

Dessert was a chocolate cake. Clara had never tasted anything so smooth and delicious.

"What kind is this?" she asked.

"Devil's food," said Mrs. Knapp.

"But I mean, what brand?"

Nettie was trying hard not to smile. "Mama makes things from scratch."

"What's scratch?" Clara asked, imagining some magic ingredient, but before the words were out, she felt foolish.

"Oh, yeah," she said quickly, "no mix." Mr. Knapp cleared his throat carefully as Clara looked in awe at Mrs. Knapp.

At Clara's house, every cake began with a store-bought box. You could tell what kind you were making by the glossy picture on the front. She tried to imagine starting with just measuring cups and—what?—flour?

"How do you get the chocolate in?" she asked, amazed.

Mr. Knapp threw his head back and laughed that booming laugh. As everyone joined in, even Clara laughed happily at herself. But she still really wondered about the chocolate.

Six

"Let's go to your house," Clara said. She could feel the early November rain beginning to seep through her jacket onto her shoulders. The droplets were blurring her glasses. It was cold. She had zipped her books inside her jacket and felt silly standing there all lumpy.

"Come on, Raz," Nettie insisted. "We can't *always* go to my house. And besides, we can use your encyclopedia for that colonial stuff."

"Your Papa just bought a brand new set!"

"Yeah, 'the best'—no pictures, and the print's so small you're bored before you read it."

Clara traced the elbow-shaped crack in the sidewalk with the toe of her saddle shoe. It was a familiar crack by now. She and Nettie spent almost every afternoon together, but they usually paused on this corner to decide between the Knapp world and the Nelson world.

"There's nothing for snacks at our house," Clara complained.

Nettie just started off toward the Nelsons'.

"It's Friday, Raz," she called back over her shoulder. "I bet your Mom's been shopping."

Mom had definitely been shopping. There were still two bags of groceries on the window seat in the front hall, and the dogs had torn open a loaf of bread, spreading crumbs and shreds of waxy paper all over the scattered shoes and galoshes. Clara hated those black galoshes. They were the rubber kind with the noisy metal buckles. Mom bought a new pair whenever Teddy's feet got bigger, and his old pairs were handed down and down till little Jubie wore them out.

Mom came hurrying down the stairs, signaling for quiet. "Hi, girls. Good day? We got home late and Jubie's still nap—" Then Mom saw the mess. "Oh, drat!"

Clara winced. The Knapps never even came close to swearing.

But Nettie just said, "Don't worry, Mrs. Nelson. We can clean it up."

"Thanks, honey. How's Patty? Haven't seen her in ages."

Patty was always with her friend Cheryl these days, but Mom didn't wait for an answer. She had already grabbed both bags of groceries and headed for the kitchen.

"I got some more peanut butter," she called, "if you

girls want a snack." They could hear cupboards open and shut. "Staying for supper tonight, Nettie?"

Once the girls got settled in the living room, Nettie actually did take out the encyclopedia. She found the section on "Colonial Life in America" and looked intently at the pictures. Occasionally she would show Clara something "neat": a whale-oil lamp or a hand-stitched sampler, a spinning wheel or an old printing press.

Clara figured this was close enough to doing their homework, at least for now. She played Oggie's banjo.

It was really Clara's banjo now, but she thought of Oggie every time she picked it up. The last day at the farm, the station wagon had been all loaded for Newingham; Dad had taken the dogs back the weekend before. Oggie hobbled out to the car, carrying the banjo in its black case. When she handed it to Clara, she just said, "Play it, Raz. Play it with all your heart. Play it for two." The car was already jam-packed, so Clara had to hold the banjo. She hugged it betweeen her knees all the way back to Newingham.

Now Nettie held out the open encyclopedia. "Look." She was pointing to a picture of a young woman knitting while a little curly-headed girl learned her ABC's from a hornbook.

"I see what you mean," Clara acknowledged. "Looks just like Patty—and Jubie."

"Me?"

Clara and Nettie hadn't heard Jubie come downstairs. She was hesitating in the doorway, sleepy-eyed.

"Why, yes, Mistress Juliana." Nettie held out the

open volume to Jubie. "Do come see. 'Tis a likeness of you and my dear sister, Goodwife Patricia."

Jubie ran forward eagerly, and soon Goodwife Lynette was making an illustrated hornbook for her enthusiastic pupil.

"A is for *apron*," Nettie declared. She took off her white cardigan sweater and tied it by the sleeves around Jubie's waist. Then she made a quick drawing in which Jubie had on a long dress, and the apron looked like the long, simple ones in the encyclopedia.

"B is for *bonnet*," Nettie continued, and began to add that to the drawing.

Jubie giggled as she pulled the sweater off her waist and plopped it on her head, doing her best to tie the sleeves under her chin.

"A is for *apron*," Clara sang, finding some chords on her banjo. "A is for *apron*; B is for *bonnet*. Your head looks silly with a sweater on it."

Jubie giggled so hard, she got Nettie and Clara going, too, and they continued to draw and clown and sing their way through the alphabet, looking up colonial ideas in the encyclopedia.

"F is for *foot warmer*."

"G is for *glassblowing*."

Every once in a while there was a commotion in the hall: The dogs followed the Little Boys outside to play; Laura, then Teddy, got home from junior high and let the dogs back in; the Little Boys burst indoors, screaming at each other as they ran upstairs to the third floor. Then Dad was home.

"Robby and Donny!" Mom hollered up the back stairs. "Time to set the table!"

Dad paused in the living-room doorway. He grinned. "Hello, Hortense," he said to Nettie, winking at Clara. After he'd gotten it straight that Nettie wasn't Patty, he made up a new name every time he greeted her. Clara wondered again why Dad never seemed so critical of kids outside the family. *Maybe that's the whole point*, she thought suddenly—*they're outside the family*.

Nettie laughed at the new name as Jubie ran to her father and corrected him earnestly.

"No, that's Goodwife Lynette!" Then she pointed to Clara. "And that's Goodwife Clara."

"Clarissa," Clara said. Her own name sounded too ordinary.

Jubie stood tall and put her hands on her hips. "And I'm Miss Dress Julie-On-A," she declared proudly.

Dad chuckled as he turned toward the kitchen.

"Robby and Donny Nelson!" Mom yelled again. "Get down here!" In Newingham, it seemed, Mom was always impatient. And always shouting.

As one of the Little Boys yelled a weak "Coming!" from the third floor, Clara could hear Dad in the kitchen, rustling his newspaper and talking at Mom in his sour tone. He was probably criticizing her for bringing up such disobedient kids. Sure enough, Clara could hear the defensive tone of Mom's response. Clara frowned and glanced apologetically at Nettie.

"Play another song," Nettie urged, and she held Clara's gaze for a second.

But as Robby and Donny finally came clomping down the stairs, Clara put her banjo aside and left the living room. She'd been teaching the Little Boys how to set the table right. They just threw everything on the old way if she wasn't there.

Robby was already marching around the outside of the dining room making airplane noises as he sailed straw placemats toward the table. Little Donny was valiantly trying to slap each one before it sailed right off onto the floor. Then he'd run and get a plate from the stack at the end of the table and plunk it down wherever the mat had landed.

"Come on," said Clara. She went around straightening everything.

Robby opened a drawer in the pantry and pawed through the jumble of silverware. "Do we need knives?" he yelled to Mom.

"Nope—it's just hamburg and peas."

Clara grabbed for the knives anyway. "Some people cut up their hamburgers," she half whispered to Robby.

"Mom got rolls," Robby whined.

"Here, Donny." Clara set a stack of little bread plates on the table. "Put one of these at the top of each knife, okay?"

"What for?" Donny was whining now, too.

"The bread," Clara said impatiently, "the rolls."

"That's dumb," said Robby. "The rolls go on the hamburg."

"Do as I say!" Clara said, seething with frustration.

"Don't tell me what to do!"

"*Somebody's* gotta tell you how to do things *right* around here *once* in awhile!"

"Shut up!" Robby said. "You're not a grown-up!"

"Mo-om," Donny piped up, heading for the kitchen, "Robby said, 'shut up'!"

Robby had grabbed some paper napkins and was slapping them around at each place. Clara flounced around after him.

"You have to *fold* them!" she scolded, folding them herself.

"That's dumb!"

"You're dumb yourself!"

"Clara Sperry Nelson!" Mom stood in the doorway with a greasy spatula in her hand. "Don't speak that way to your brother!"

"He won't do it *right!*"

Mom's face tightened sharply. "Nobody around here does anything right, as far as you and some others are concerned. So just get out of the way and let us muddle through the wrong way! Do you hear?"

Clara couldn't believe Mom was *that* angry. "Come on, Mom. I was just—"

"Get out, I said! Robby and Donny can finish the table. After dinner, you can wash the dishes *exactly right*, if you're so perfect!" Mom wheeled around and disappeared back into the kitchen. They could hear her slamming the pots and pans. Dad's newspaper rustled, but he didn't speak.

Clara felt as though she'd run smack into a tornado

that hadn't even been forecast. Robby and Donny were standing there as if stuck in a statues game.

"We'll do it your way, Raz," said Robby.

Clara felt tears behind her eyes.

"Never mind," she said. She lifted her glasses to swipe at her face with the napkin she'd been about to fold. She sat down at the place she'd been about to straighten— Dad's place at the head of the table. As Robby and Donny moved glumly along, trying to fold the rest of the napkins, Clara surveyed the dull, sloppy table. She tried to imagine it glittering with polished silver on a glossy white cloth. She tried to imagine a gentle, soft-spoken woman at the other end and booming laughter erupting from this end. The tears came. She swiped at them again, crumpled the napkin into a damp wad, and placed it exactly in the center of Dad's plate.

Then she heard some loud, wild banjo chords from the living room—Nettie, for sure. Jubie came running in and tugged at one of Clara's hands with both of hers. "Come on," she said urgently. "We need you! She's stuck on Q!"

"Q is for *quilting bee*," Clara said almost automatically, and she let Jubie pull her out of the dismal dining room.

"Come on," Jubie kept saying, "Come on, Goodwife Raz!"

Someone had given Dad a fresh napkin before they all got to the table.

Mom paid special attention to Clara during supper,

telling her that Oggie had called and asked how the banjo playing was going. Clara knew Mom was apologizing, and accepted by offering to do the dishes as if it were a new idea. Nettie helped, of course, singing "You Are My Sunshine" at the top of her lungs, so that even Dad, sitting as he often did at the kitchen table, hummed along from behind his newspaper.

Part III

WINTER
1958-1959
Newingham

Seven

It was the bleak, empty week between Christmas and
New Year's. Clara sat in the Knapps' peaceful kitchen.
Her whole family had gone skiing for the day, but she
had pleaded to stay at Nettie's.

"She's over there too much," Dad had said to Mom
as if Clara hadn't been standing right there in front of
him.

Mom had shrugged. "They seem glad to have her."

Hard for him to imagine, Clara had thought, yet not
dared to say.

But this time she had won.

Now she sat with her banjo and watched Nettie draw
with broad, magical strokes on rough paper. Four bread

pans sat on the wooden table. Bulges were beginning to show under the damp dish towels that covered them. Clara felt warm and rescued. She could imagine Dad herding the Little Kids up the beginners' ski slope, their noses running, their fingers numb.

"You're not cold!" he'd be saying. "Stop complaining."

"I want some cocoa," little Jubie would be saying, and tears would be starting to trail down across her bright red cheeks.

"Stop crying," Dad would say.

"I'm not," Jubie would insist, sidestepping up the slope with greater determination. "The wind just makes my eyes cry."

Laura would be dawdling near the bottom of the slope among what Dad called the "snow bunnies"—women in pastel parkas and fluffy white hats who wore lots of lipstick; they fell all the time, and had to be helped up by the handsome ski-patrol men.

Teddy was probably in the men's room in the warming hut, sitting on the closed toilet with a book.

Mom would ski a few runs and then come take over with the Little Kids. Jubie would finally get her cocoa.

"Let's make cocoa," Clara suggested to Nettie.

"I'll make it," said Patty, just coming in with her knitting.

"Nice service here!" said Nettie. She ducked her head and grabbed at her own braid without quite escaping Patty's tug.

Smiling as Nettie laughed, Patty dropped her knitting

on a chair and reached into the refrigerator for some milk. The Knapps made cocoa with real milk and chocolate, not hot water poured over a packet of mysterious powder.

Clara was just getting up to fetch the sugar when Mrs. Knapp swept in and, with one familiar motion, took her ironed apron from its hook, slipped it over her head, and tied it neatly around her waist.

"I'm sorry, girls," she said in her soft, pleasant drawl. "I need my kitchen back."

"We were just making cocoa," Nettie protested.

Patty put the milk away.

"I'll make it for you a little later," Mrs. Knapp offered. She was alreading pulling out a mixing bowl, the flour canister, her rolling pin. "The bread's risen. I want to bake this pie now, too."

Nettie gathered her drawings, but with exaggerated slowness. Mrs. Knapp didn't seem to notice. She just pushed at the papers absently, making room for her work. "Play upstairs, all right, girls? And could you please straighten up in the attic a little? You left a lot of clothes out."

The third floor of the Knapps' house was not really an attic like Oggie's. It had a spare bedroom—rarely used but always shining dustless—and a tiny bathroom under the eaves. But it also had a storage room, where there were old trunks, a faded velvet couch, and elegant bureaus with handles missing or drawers that stuck. In the storage room, there was even a little dust. Here the three girls had pushed aside boxes of books and arranged chairs to face the couch. Here they often sat, pretending to be famous, or foreign, or old-fashioned, while Nettie drew, and Patty knit, and Clara plucked contentedly at her banjo.

The clothes in these trunks could not match the selection in Oggie's attic, but there were a few long skirts and several white blouses. The girls took their time. They tried different combinations, assisted and advised each other, until finally Goodwife Lynette and Goodwife Clarissa and Goodwife Patricia stood in front of the long mirror that leaned against the chimney in the storage room. Clara stood a little to the side so she wouldn't have to see herself as she pinned up her scraggly braids. She watched the twins twist their thick brown hair into fancy knots.

"Got any extra knitting needles?" Nettie asked her sister, and Patty helped her crisscross two shiny blue needles through her elegant hair.

"You look Japanese," said Clara, stepping forward to adjust one of the needles. She saw herself unexpectedly in the mirror: Her glasses had slipped down on her nose, and the bristly ends of her braids were sticking straight up like paintbrushes. "And I look like a rooster," she said angrily. She grabbed at the bobby pins and flung them onto a nearby bureau. "Drat!" She felt wonderfully bold almost swearing in the Knapps' house.

"Mayhaps I'll go fix that tea now," said Patty. The smell of baking bread had reached them on the third floor, and that usually meant Mrs. Knapp would soon pull the finished loaves from the oven. Patty lifted the hem of her skirt daintily as she headed for the stairs.

Nettie used her colonial voice. "Please to let *me* fix your hair, Clarissa dear." She rummaged in Patty's knitting for a length of yarn, then pulled Clara toward the velvet couch. Clara sat sideways in front of her friend and felt her frustration dissolve as those lively hands bound the disobedient braids into a soft curve across the back of her neck. She sighed. She could smell the pie, now, too, and she was pretty sure it was apple.

It was getting dark. Clara thought of the Little Kids, at last allowed to shiver toward home and warmth, their numb toes beginning to sting painfully inside their ski boots. She reached forward and turned on the lamp at the end of the couch. Beyond the circle of lamplight, the outlying spaces under the eaves turned suddenly mysterious and cavelike, swallowing in shadow the piles of books and boxes, the fancy bureaus in disrepair.

"There, Clarissa dear," Nettie said with satisfaction. She turned toward the trunk they used as a table and shuffled through her pages of drawings for a blank sheet.

Clara reached for her banjo. "Oops," she said. "I don't think they had banjos back then."

"Why, Goodwife Clarissa," Nettie cooed, "I'm so glad you brought your dulcimer."

Clara smiled. She bet that if the Knapps had a television—or a flying saucer, for that matter—Nettie would find a way to make it fit into their games.

Patty came in with a tray of cocoa, and suddenly the whole room seemed moist with the smell of steaming chocolate.

"Mama said no bread—it's almost time for supper."

"Such a lovely tea service, Patricia dear." Nettie pushed her drawings unceremoniously onto the floor to make room on the trunk for the cocoa. "I made some crumpets this morning. I'll just go fetch them." And with a swish of her long skirt, she left the storage room and hurried down the stairs. As Nettie shut the door that closed off the third floor, Clara heard that warm, mischievous giggle echo in the second-floor hallway.

Clara could easily imagine the scene in the kitchen: Nettie would ramble on excitedly with some earnest story—maybe that they were rehearsing a play about colonial times, and needed a prop for the crumpets. Mrs. Knapp wouldn't be the least bit fooled, but a smile would come into her eyes, and she'd slice some bread for Nettie.

Clara bent over her banjo, concentrating hard on the frailing for "Amazing Grace." She glanced up at Patty, whose glance was just flickering back to her knitting. The separate clicking rhythm of the needles jumbled awkwardly with the twang of the banjo strings.

Then Nettie was back in the doorway, her face flushed. She plunked a plate down on the table: three thick slices of fresh, hot bread absolutely *afloat* with butter.

"Crumpets anyone?" And she giggled an uncolonial giggle. She plopped down on the couch. "I've got a headache," she said abruptly.

"Try some of this lovely tea, my dear." Patty handed Nettie a cup of cocoa.

"Is there any aspirin up here?" Clara asked.

Nettie got up to go look, and almost seemed to totter. Patty reached up to steady her. "Would you like some help, Lynette dear?"

"You look pale," Clara said, following Nettie into the bathroom.

"No aspirin," Nettie concluded, closing the mirrored door to the medicine cabinet.

Patty joined them with her own voice. "Maybe it's the knitting needles, or your hair's too tight."

Nettie seemed to be leaning for support on the sink, so Clara took out the knitting needles and hairpins to let Nettie's hair down. Such beautiful, rich hair. Clara tried not to look at her own face next to Nettie's in the little mirror. She would see the mousy eyes behind the glasses, the pathetic thin hair already falling down, despite Nettie's magic.

"It still really hurts," Nettie said weakly, and suddenly Clara realized her friend looked awful. Patty had noticed it, too.

"Come, my dear," Patty coaxed, "come back to the parlor and rest yourself on the settee. I'll send for the doctor."

As Patty guided her sister back into the storeroom, Clara asked if she should check downstairs for aspirin, but then Nettie collapsed onto a big, dome-lidded trunk and slid to the floor. Patty and Clara both laughed awkwardly, but there was no giggle from Nettie. Clara ran to her.

"Mama!" Patty yelled. "Mama!" But they always

closed the door at the bottom of the attic stairs. Mrs. Knapp would still be in the kitchen, making preparations for dinner.

"Rub her hand," Patty half whispered, looking as scared as Clara was. Clara was grateful for something to do. They propped Nettie's back against the trunk. Her face was gray, but her eyes were open. "Rub her hand," Patty said again. "I'll go get Mama."

Clara rubbed Nettie's limp hand. She knew it was silly in any medical sense, but it kept her there—very much there—for her friend. She was frightened past anything she'd known. Nettie seemed barely conscious, muttering some. Then she said distinctly, "I'm going to die."

"No you're not," Clara answered firmly, but Nettie seemed far away, and her dark eyes had focused on something Clara couldn't see.

"I'm going to die," Nettie said again. "Or am I?"

Eight

"Something terrible's happened to Nettie."

Clara and Patty could hear Mrs. Knapp on the telephone in the hall. They sat stiffly on the living-room couch pretending not to listen. They were still in their long skirts. Clara folded her hands and lowered her eyes as if in church. She could feel Patty's presence like the next person over in the pew—they were there together, but they couldn't turn to each other, or talk even in whispers. Knitting or playing the banjo would be out of the question—and anyway, they'd left all that upstairs on the old velvet couch.

By now it was truly dark outside, and the Christmas tree in the corner looked sad and drab without its lights on. Mr. Knapp had come home and was upstairs with Nettie. The doctor was expected any minute.

Mrs. Knapp had called Clara's house several times before. It had scared Clara to hear her dial and dial, wait in silence, dial again a few minutes later.

At last the Nelsons were home. Clara could imagine her family spilling in from skiing, the Little Kids whining, Laura probably pouting, Teddy in a fog when the phone rang. Mom would answer the phone with annoyance, expecting nothing important. She'd be crooking the receiver under her chin, putting down handfuls of wet mittens, and opening the fridge to see what there might be for supper.

"Something terrible's happened to Nettie," Mrs. Knapp repeated. "Clara will have to go home right away."

Clara winced and glanced at Patty. Patty was already looking at Clara. For just a moment, those two huge brown eyes widened with terror and loneliness. Clara almost opened her arms into a hug, but Patty looked away.

Dad arrived soon after the doctor. Clara's stomach squirmed with embarrassment to see her own father standing there, short and awkward, on the Knapps' elegant rug. He was still wearing his stretchy ski pants.

"Patty can come stay with us," he suggested.

Mrs. Knapp could hardly speak. Wisps of hair had fallen from her glossy, graying bun and floated unnoticed around her anguished face. "Would you like a glass of sherry?" she asked.

"I'll wait outside and signal the ambulance," Dad

offered, and Mrs. Knapp at last felt free to go back upstairs to Nettie.

Patty followed to pack some clothes.

Clara waited in the car with Dad. He had the motor running and the headlights on. He peered straight ahead as if to say his concentration should not be interrupted. Clara's mind swirled with questions she couldn't ask: *Why didn't Mom come to get me? Mom would talk to me. Mom would tell me what's wrong with Nettie. What's* wrong *with Nettie? Why did Nettie say that about dying? Why can't I go say good-bye? How long will Patty stay? Oh, please,* please, *somebody tell me what's wrong with Nettie!*

Patty came out with her little twin suitcase. (Were they packing Nettie's for the hospital?) She climbed into the back seat and joined in the silence.

The ambulance came up the street with lights flashing, but no siren. Dad signaled with his headlights and got out to say something to the driver. Why did Nettie need an ambulance? Last year, Clara had been rushed to the hospital after her appendix ruptured. She had gone in her pajamas, wrapped in a quilt. But Mom had driven her. Why did Nettie need an ambulance?

Now Dad got back into the car. As they drove away, Clara saw the ambulance driver and another man carry a stretcher in through the Knapps' front door. They didn't even knock or ring the bell.

The Nelsons' house was all lit up.

"Looks like a damn lighthouse," Dad grumbled.

The Little Kids came running into the hallway, stumbling over strewn galoshes and ski boots. "Raz!" "Hi, Raz!" "Raz's home!" The Little Boys held back when they saw Patty, but Jubie threw herself straight at Clara, locking her arms around Clara's neck, then wrapping her little legs around Clara's waist as Clara lifted her. Suddenly the tears burned in Clara's eyes and she could not stop them. She bent her head to wipe them unnoticed on Jubie's shirt.

Mom came in from the kitchen and gave Patty a hug, but Patty was still holding the twin suitcase, and her arms stayed at her sides.

"Come on," Mom said. "I bet you two haven't eaten. There's plenty of stew left."

Jubie jumped down and pulled Clara after their mother. "Guess what, Raz! Mom bought us cocoa in the warming hut!"

Dad was already in the kitchen, ladling out two crockery bowls of stew.

"Every light in the house is on," he complained to Mom.

Mom sent the Little Kids upstairs to get ready for bed. "And turn out a few lights while you're at it," she called after them.

Mom did dishes while the girls ate silently, and when they'd finished, she didn't even ask them to help.

Later, when Clara and Patty turned out the light and lay silent, one on each side of Clara's wide, high bed, Mom came to tuck them in as if they were little like Jubie.

She went to Patty's side and gave her a kiss. "Sleep

well," she said. "We'll know more tomorrow. You can just stay here with us, okay? Nettie's going to be all right."

Then Mom came around to Clara's side and sat on the bed to give her a hug. "Good-night, Raz. You get some sleep and you two can have a fun day tomorrow. I'm sure Nettie's going to be all right." Mom hugged her again.

Clara didn't think she'd ever sleep. Her mind felt cramped and dark, like the long tunnel of the last few hours, and voices kept echoing from its shadows.

"I'm going to die . . . or am I?"

"Something terrible's happened to Nettie."

"A fun day tomorrow." Maybe Mom would let them go to the movies. Maybe she'd let them make fudge to send to Nettie in the hospital.

But what's wrong with Nettie? "Nettie's going to be all right." *But what's wrong?* "A fun day tomorrow."

Nettie's going to be all right.

Nettie's going to be . . .

Nettie's . . .

going . . .

Patty stayed the next day, and the next. Nettie was in a coma, Mom explained. Like being in a deep sleep. The doctors were doing tests. Mr. and Mrs. Knapp were practically living at the hospital. They called Patty. They said they'd be home soon.

But Patty stayed the next day, too.

Dad took Teddy and Laura and the Little Kids skiing for the New Year's holiday. Usually the whole family went—they stayed overnight with old college friends of

Dad's who got drunk on New Year's Eve. Their kids went to private school and acted all snobby toward public-school kids like the Nelsons. Clara hated New Year's Eve.

But this time, Mom had stayed behind with her and Patty. *Rescued again*, Clara thought. And it was fun having a live-in friend.

Mom had rummaged in the storage closet for her box of yarns and knitting needles, and now both girls were working on new scarves. Clara's was bright purple; Patty's was blue, like the one she'd left half-finished at home. Sometimes Clara's busy hands itched for her banjo, but then she would picture it again, leaning against the velvet couch, where she'd left it when Nettie needed aspirin. She couldn't imagine going back into that room to get it.

She bent her head to concentrate harder on her knitting.

"Drat!" she said, and Patty looked up, startled. They were sitting cross-legged on Clara's bed.

"Goofed *again*," Clara explained. In frustration, she started pulling out the last few rows. Then it seemed kind of fun, the way the purple yarn unraveled all kinky and curly, and she pulled out row after row, just to watch it jump and twirl.

"This is neat!" she said, and giggled.

Suddenly, amazingly, Patty was pulling out her work, too, and then Clara pulled out some of Patty's and Patty pulled out some of Clara's, and they were giggling and grabbing at each other's yarn until their needles were bare and they could not stop laughing. Heaps of purple and blue yarn tangled with each other on the knobbly white bedspread.

"Catch!" Clara said breathlessly, grabbing a spare ball of yarn from Mom's box and tossing it to Patty. They stood on opposite sides of the bed and threw the ball back and forth, doubling over in spasms of laughter as it unwound into tangled patterns over everything. Then they grabbed another ball, several. They caromed the balls off the ceiling, bringing down flecks of peeled paint. They rolled the balls under the bed, collecting dust like cotton candy. They sprawled under the bed to chase them; they sprawled on top of the bed, laughing and laughing till their stomachs ached.

"Girls!" Mom called up the stairs. They looked at each other and pulled their lips tight to keep from laughing out loud again. "Girls? If you're going to that matinee, we'd better leave now!"

They heaped all the rainbow tangles of yarn onto the bed, and their giggles subsided like echoes.

"Girls?"

"We're coming!" Clara called. This New Year's Eve felt more like her birthday or something. Only last week, Mom had said this movie was junk; now she was driving them there, and paying, too. Then they were going to have steak for supper, stay up till midnight, maybe go next door in their nightgowns to watch Times Square on television. This big house felt cozy when she had all Mom's attention.

Clara and Patty walked home from the movie in the early dusk. A light snow was falling, a sprinkle of clean whiteness over the old, drab snow. It reminded Clara of Mrs. Knapp sifting confectioner's sugar in a lacy pattern over one of her spice cakes.

As they took off their coats in the hallway at home, Mom came down the stairs, smiling.

"Guess what *I've* been doing while you were gone," she said. She pretended to be holding something in each hand, circling one around the other as she went on in a silly, squeaky voice: "Winding and winding and winding up lit-tle balls of yarn!"

Patty smiled, a little embarrassed, but Clara felt a sudden rush of panic. Why wasn't Mom angry? Or at least annoyed! She should be sternly telling them to untangle that mess before supper. Why was she being so careful of them? She was acting like Mrs. Knapp!

"Come help me cook supper," Mom said then, and Clara felt a little better.

Right after supper, Mom sent them upstairs to get ready for bed—they could spend the evening in their nightgowns and go to bed whenever they got tired. Clara was on the way back from brushing her teeth when the doorbell rang. She leaned over the upstairs railing as Mom opened the front door and let in a rush of cold air.

Mr. and Mrs. Knapp were standing there, side by side. Clara suddenly noticed the usual mess in the hallway, and wished she'd cleaned it up. Patty came up behind her as Mr. Knapp spoke solemnly to Mom.

"We've come to get Patty."

"What about Nettie?" Patty asked pleadingly. Her parents looked up the stairs, surprised. Mom was still holding the door open.

"She can't come home yet, honey," said Mrs. Knapp. Her voice was infinitely gentle. "It's okay. We'll be there with you."

"I want to stay here," Patty said weakly.

"Clara," said Mom in her no-nonsense tone, "help Patty get her things together." Then she turned to the Knapps as if the girls were already forgotten. "Come on in and sit down."

As Patty left with her parents, Clara said good-bye from the top of the stairs. Patty had her winter coat pulled over her nightgown, and she looked small and sad. Clara felt the house grow huge and empty.

Mom shut the door and turned to come up the stairs. She held one arm across her stomach, and the closer she got to Clara, the more twisted and pale her face looked. Was she going to collapse now, too?

"Mom, are you okay?"

Mom stopped a few steps before the top and held on tightly to the banister. Her face was even with Clara's.

"When they came to the door without calling like that. . . ." Mom's voice was wobbling. She swallowed and went on in almost a whisper. "When they came to the door without calling like that, I thought for sure Nettie was dead!"

Nine

Clara stood stunned. She stared at her mother. There was a distant echo somewhere: "I'm going to die. . . ." But then Clara's mind began to churn out another sentence, over and over.

Nettie's going to be all right.

Then Clara heard herself shout it: "Nettie's going to be all right!" She shouted it at her mother, whose face was still right there in front of her. "You said Nettie's going to be all right! Mom, you *said*!"

Mom came up the last few steps and surrounded Clara in a hug. Clara burst at last into angry, terrified tears.

"Oh, Raz," was all Mom said.

"She *can't* die, Mom, she *can't*! She's coming back, I *know* she is!"

"I hope so with all my heart, honey, but she's very sick. She's very, very sick, and it's no use pretending otherwise."

"But what's *wrong*?"

Clara sobbed without trying to stop. She let her mother guide her toward her room. She was glad to be crying at last, glad to feel her head on the pillow and her mother's hand stroking her hair. Mom took off Clara's glasses and turned out the light. A warm glow from the hallway softened the darkness. In moments when Clara's crying calmed a bit, her mother talked gently about Nettie.

"They say a blood vessel broke in the back of her brain. It's very rare, and they don't know why it happens. It's not contagious, honey, but it is *very* serious. They're doing everything they can, Raz, I promise." Mom breathed in sharply. "And she's not in any pain, honey. That's a blessing, at least."

Mom was silent for a time.

"They're feeding her intravenously—remember the needle in your arm when you were in the hospital?"

Clara nodded slightly, keeping her eyes closed. She could see the fuzzy image of the plastic bag hanging over her hospital bed, dripping fluid through a tube into her arm. Sometimes, half dreaming, she had thought the bag was swelling, threatening to explode like a bomb. Her forearm with the needle in it was tied to a board and to the bed. She would be trapped there when the explosion came.

Clara squeezed her eyes more tightly shut to scatter the menacing image. She didn't want to remember anything. She just wanted Mom to keep talking and stroking her hair.

"Nettie's coming back," she said weakly.

"Oh, Raz, I hope so." For a moment Mom's hand on Clara's hair seemed to stroke too fast and too hard. "But the bleeding's in her brain, honey. It can cause damage, Raz, and our brains just don't mend that easily."

Clara opened her swollen eyes. Even if she'd had her glasses on, her tears would have made the dark world foggy. But for just a second she saw Nettie's face, as clear as in a well-lit photograph. Nettie was giggling that rich, warm giggle—Clara could tell, because those wide, brown eyes were dancing. There was an echo from somewhere: ". . . or am I?"

"Nettie's coming back!" Clara shouted suddenly, and she pounded her pillow with her fist.

But when Christmas vacation ended, Nettie was still in a coma. It had been a week since her collapse, a week that seemed to Clara like miles and miles of hollow years.

Nettie's desk at school was empty. It looked like a big hole right in the middle of everything. Miss Ziff took Clara aside and asked sympathetically about Nettie.

"She's really sick," Clara explained, "but she's going to be all right." Clara didn't mention the other things Mom had slowly been telling her—about the breathing tube, and the other tube. If Miss Ziff knew all that, she might think Nettie wasn't coming back.

All the other kids were buzzing about their holiday gifts, or about who went where for a New Year's party. Clara felt lost in the midst of them. She and Patty spent recess together. They walked the deep snow beyond the cleared blacktop, and their other friends left them alone.

Clara walked home with Patty that afternoon—and the next, and the next. They didn't even pause at the corner with the elbow-crack in the sidewalk. They went straight to the Knapps'. They sat in the living room by the faded Christmas tree and knitted. They made fudge, and imagined they were making it for Nettie.

After a few days, Mrs. Knapp asked Patty to take the ornaments off the Christmas tree.

"Okay, Mama," said Patty, but then she noticed a mistake several rows back in her knitting, and she worked to fix it until Mrs. Knapp reappeared and reminded her about the tree.

Clara got up to help.

"Let's check the fudge first," said Patty. The fudge had cooled. Patty got out a silver candy dish and set to polishing it. When Mrs. Knapp came down to take her chicken potpie out of the oven, Clara half expected her to get annoyed. *Mom* would have been annoyed. But Mrs. Knapp didn't even mention the tree.

Clara helped Patty spread a clean, checkered tablecloth over the kitchen table so that they could set it. It would be just the three of them again. Mr. Knapp always stopped at the hospital after work and didn't get home till late. Mrs. Knapp had made a separate pie for him— she'd take it hot from the oven when he got home.

After school the next day, Mrs. Knapp sounded surprisingly firm when she mentioned the tree. "It's time to take it down, Patty. It's dropping its needles. I'm sure Clara won't mind helping."

Clara jumped up. She was eager to have something to do, anything to do, but then Patty blurted out, "What about Nettie?"

For just a brief second, there was utter silence, an empty silence that filled the room.

Then Mrs. Knapp answered Patty gently. "She won't be home that soon, honey. We've left the tree up as long as we could." Mrs. Knapp turned and left. She seemed in a hurry.

When the last Christmas ornament was nestled in the tissue paper in its carefully labeled box, Patty went behind the tree to begin unclipping the lights. Clara couldn't see her face, and her voice was whispery: "What's wrong with Nettie—do you know?"

Clara sighed. "I don't understand it, either. It's so weird."

"But what *is* it? Mama and Papa just say I can't catch it."

Suddenly Clara realized what Patty was asking. "You mean you don't know *anything*?"

"They never talk about it."

Clara peered through the dry, prickly branches of the forlorn spruce tree. "Do you know about the blood vessel, about her brain?"

"Her *brain*? No, nothing." Patty emerged from behind

the tree and looked straight at Clara. Her wide, brown eyes were pleading.

"Let's go for a walk," Clara said.

Carefully, Clara told Patty everything Mom had told her—about the broken blood vessel, and what the doctors were doing. Patty kept her eyes on the icy sidewalk and seemed to listen with her whole body.

"They have to be sure she can breathe okay," Clara said softly, "because she can't cough or anything. So they put a breathing tube in her throat—just till she gets conscious again."

The other tube was harder to explain.

"The danger is from the spinal fluid in her brain— from the pressure. I mean, I guess we all have the fluid, but it's supposed to circulate—or get absorbed or something—and the bleeding somehow blocked it, so it just builds up. They had to put a tube from her brain to her heart—spinal fluid's almost like blood, I guess, without the red. They call the tube a shunt." Clara hesitated, then added, "Nettie will have some scars when she comes back." She glanced sideways and was silent.

Slowly, keeping her eyes down, Patty began asking questions, and Clara tried to explain as Mom had explained to her. Patty seemed so starved for information that Clara felt angrier and angrier at Mr. and Mrs. Knapp. Why wouldn't they tell her the truth? From now on, Clara promised, she'd bring Patty all the news as soon as she heard it from Mom.

*   *   *

But there was no news at all. Nettie was in a coma.

There was no news through the end of January. Clara was practically living at the Knapps'. She and Patty finished their scarves and started new ones.

There was no news by February vacation. Dad put his foot down this time, and Clara had to go skiing with the family all week. Some vacation. Patty called right after the Nelsons got home, but there was still no news. Nettie was in a coma.

When Clara got to school the next morning, she noticed right away that Nettie's desk was gone. She decided that she really hated Miss Ziff.

When Miss Ziff sat and crossed her legs in front of the class, her straight skirt rode up over her knees, and Clara could see a wide run in her stocking, right over her kneecap. The skin bulged in whitened bumps through the holes between the cross-threads. Miss Ziff had tried to stop the run with pink nail polish like the stuff on her fingernails, but that just made it look more like a nasty, ugly scar.

What would Nettie's scars be like?

"Clara?"

Clara had no idea what Miss Ziff's question had been. "I don't know," she said.

"You don't have to be right," Miss Ziff coaxed. "Just give it a try."

"I *said* I don't know." Clara couldn't believe how brazen she sounded.

"Watch your tone, Clara Nelson," Miss Ziff warned, but she went on to someone else. Clara knew she was lucky. Miss Ziff was easy on mistakes, or even disruptions, but she really hated to be sassed.

That afternoon, Clara noticed the nasty run again. She doodled on her spelling paper beside the dumb practice sentences Miss Ziff was dictating.

"*Distract.* Loud noises may *distract* us from our work."

Clara thought about scars, about her own appendix scar, about being in the hospital herself. "You nearly died," her mother had told her later, but Clara only remembered calling the nurses that night, afraid they'd be mad at her for complaining. And then those weird dreams.

"*Earnest,*" Miss Ziff dictated. "She made an *earnest* attempt to understand."

After the night Clara nearly died, Dad even came to visit her. He stopped in on his way home from work. One time he helped her put her glasses on and used the back of his gold pocket watch to show her what she looked like with tubes down her throat and in her nose. They laughed together, because the watch reflected her like a fun house mirror, all squiggly and distorted. "You'll be fine in no time, Raz," Dad said. Clara couldn't remember if he'd ever called her Raz before or since.

"Tim York!" Miss Ziff was saying. "Please put those doodles away and pay attention."

Clara glanced at where Nettie's desk had been. "Lots of us were doodling," Clara burst out. She tried to sound all cheerful, the way Nettie would, but she was angry, and it just came out rude. "You always pick on Tim."

Miss Ziff looked at Clara with a mixture of fury and

surprise. She spoke very slowly: "Well, Clara Nelson. Perhaps you can stay after school today, and we can have a little talk about that."

But after school, Miss Ziff didn't talk. She just sat at her desk at the back of the room and made Clara sit at hers, facing front.

Then Miss Ziff noticed Patty waiting outside on the swings. "You go on home, Patty," she called out the door. "Clara's staying after."

Clara felt her eyes go hot, and she turned a bit in her chair to be sure that Miss Ziff wouldn't get the satisfaction of seeing her cry. She thought of offering to wash the blackboards or water the plants, but she figured her voice would be too shaky. Then she heard Miss Ziff open a window and call loudly, "Go on, Patty. Don't wait for Clara. She's going to be here a long time." And the window clicked shut again.

Suddenly Clara's tears dried up, as if a hot wind had hit them. She folded her arms and focused her thoughts: *I hate her. I hate her.* She tried to imagine the rest of the afternoon: sitting there in silence, walking home in the winter darkness, having to explain. But the more she felt like crying, the more she was determined not to—like when Dad scolded her in front of friends. She tightened her arms across her chest. *I hate her. I hate her.*

Finally Miss Ziff called Clara to the back of the room. Clara willed her face into a blank stare and concentrated on the pencil in the teacher's hand. Miss Ziff tapped the pencil on the blotter as she lectured. She slid her fingers down the length of it. Then she flipped it, tapped it again, slid her fingers down it again. Point end. Eraser end. Point end. Eraser end.

"... very smart girl, Clara ..."

Point end. Eraser end.

"... too big for your britches these days ..."

Point end. Eraser end.

"... losing Nettie must be hard ..."

Nettie's coming back! Eraser end.

"... I'm sure we all miss her ..."

Don't you dare *talk about Nettie!*

"... still no excuse to ..."

Clara could not help it. She was sobbing. Miss Ziff looked surprised and stopped talking in the middle of a sentence. She put down her pencil and handed Clara a Kleenex.

"I'm sorry, Clara. I didn't realize ..."

Clara just sobbed and blew her nose.

"You go on home now, Clara. And no more rudeness, okay?"

Clara didn't even bother to button her coat till she was out in the empty playground. It was cold and gray and windy. She scuffed her galoshes on the icy blacktop. The walk ahead seemed like a lonely, impossible trek.

Then, as she rounded the end of the school building, there was Patty, waiting on the path toward home. Patty seemed matter-of-fact, but something joyous jumped inside Clara, like when she'd gotten home from the hospital last year and Jubie had run headlong into her arms yelling "Raz! Raz! Raz!" Robby and Donny had jumped up and down, and even Laura and Teddy had been there in the front hall to welcome her. Even Laura and Teddy had given her big hugs and seemed really glad to see her.

Now Patty just smiled. "Miss Ziff can be mean, huh?"

"I guess it was kind of my fault," Clara confessed, and she told the whole story to Patty as they walked to the Knapps'.

By the time Clara got home for supper that night, staying after didn't seem so terrible anymore. She had a minute alone in the kitchen with Mom, and was just going to tell her about Miss Ziff when Mom said solemnly, "I talked to Mrs. Knapp today."

Ten

Clara waited until after school to tell Patty what Mom had said. Somehow Patty knew there was news, but she waited, too. They walked home with the February wind in their faces. Miss Ziff had been strangely gentle toward Clara that day. Miss Ziff had even been nice to Tim York. But Nettie's desk was still gone.

Mrs. Knapp spent every day and some nights at the hospital, but she was always in the kitchen when Patty and Clara got home. She fussed a little over their snack. Clara watched her closely this time as she dished out some apple pie. How could she know what Clara knew and not tell Patty? Clara felt a rush of anger. Mrs. Knapp didn't even look more upset than usual—tired, maybe. But these days, she always looked tired.

"There's ice cream," Mrs. Knapp said. That was unusual—Clara figured Mrs. Knapp didn't serve much ice cream because she didn't make her own from scratch.

Patty rummaged in the utensil drawer for the special scoop. They had one with a lever, just like the ones at ice-cream shops. Nettie had liked to use it for rice, for peas—she'd even tried it on peanut butter.

Now when Patty pressed the lever, the little gears jammed. They jammed when Clara tried, too.

Patty half smiled with annoyance. "Nettie must have broken it."

Mrs. Knapp was at the sink washing the pie plate. She bent her head. "I'm glad Nettie enjoyed it while she could." She sounded sad and lost, but Clara wanted to shake her for sounding hopeless, too.

Nettie's coming back, Clara wanted to shout. But instead, she shoved her pie and ice cream sloppily into her mouth, then waited for Patty to finish.

Finally, Patty and Clara were upstairs in the twins' room, with the door closed. They sat cross-legged on the beds and faced each other.

"It's weird," said Clara at last. "It's really weird."

Patty just waited.

Clara took a deep breath. "They've cooled her down."

She immediately regretted starting that way. Patty's big eyes widened with terror. How had Mom started? How had Mom explained it?

"It's okay," she started again. "But the shunt wasn't

working right, and some pressure built up in her brain again, and there's another doctor involved now." Clara could hear she wasn't making sense. She stopped and tried to order her thoughts.

Patty got up to get her knitting and sat back down on the bed, but this time she sat on the pillow and propped her back against the wall. She wasn't looking at Clara anymore.

"There's something about how the pressure makes it hard for oxygen to get to her brain. If they cool her down, her brain doesn't have to work so hard—it doesn't need as much oxygen." This didn't sound as reassuring as Clara wanted it to. "The cooling doesn't do Nettie any harm," she added. "It's sort of like a short hibernation, Mom says, and it prevents damage."

Patty had made a mistake in her knitting, and she lowered her head to concentrate on fixing it.

"I know it sounds really weird, but Mom says they just use ice packs under her arms and all, and a drug so her body won't shiver and warm itself up. They've already put in a new shunt, and the cooling's just till the fluid drains again."

Then Clara realized that Patty was crying. Silently. A few tears dropped on the gray yarn, but Patty just kept going, knitting them right into the scarf. Clara stopped talking and waited.

"Sounds like she's already dead," Patty mumbled. A big tear got stuck on her upper lip and she wiped it away as if she were mad at it. Clara was suddenly reminded of Jubie. Jubie had wiped a tear just that way just that morning. She'd been sulking because Clara didn't have time to watch her jump off the third-to-the-bottom stair all the way to the hall rug—and standing up, too! But all Jubie needed was a hug and a tickle. Had Clara remembered to give her those?

Patty sat on the bed, drawn in as tight as her wound ball of yarn. Clara stood up and leaned over to give her a hug. Patty kept her arms positioned for knitting, but for just a moment, her head rested gratefully on Clara's shoulder.

Clara sat down on the other bed again. "Nettie's coming back," she said firmly. She took off her glasses and rubbed her eyes with the heels of her hands. She lay back on the pillow and looked at the blurred ceiling.

There was silence for a minute, except for the click of knitting needles. Clara tried to imagine being cold. Not shivery cold on her skin, but cold right through, like ice cream.

"I found a picture of you and the Little Kids," said Patty.

Clara's thoughts bumped and careened, trying to focus back to Patty and what she was saying.

"A drawing, I mean," Patty added, getting up. "Nettie's."

Clara reached for her glasses and put them back on. Was that really a dusty spiderweb at the corner of the ceiling?

"Want to see it?" Patty was already rummaging in the top drawer of Nettie's bureau.

The picture was on real drawing paper instead of Nettie's usual notebook scraps—no pale blue lines or erased math problems. And it wasn't just a sketch. Nettie had worked on this one.

"It was under her blouses."

Clara wondered what Patty was doing going through Nettie's blouses. Patty had all the same ones in her own drawer. Then Patty seemed to want to explain.

"I rearrange her clothes sometimes. Just so they don't just stay the same."

Clara was already holding the picture. The three Little Kids were crowded around Clara on the couch while she played the banjo. The Little Boys' faces were still sketchy, but Jubie's and Clara's were drawn in completely. Jubie was looking up at her big sister with that familiar worship in her eyes. Clara had her glasses on, of course, and her braids looked as skimpy as ever, but even she had to recognize that Nettie had made her look beautiful.

Nettie had drawn herself into a nearby armchair, but silly, like the sketches she always did with three broad strokes and a few giggles. The Nettie in the picture had wild hair and big bare toes, and she was drawing.

"Could I keep this?" asked Clara.

"She liked yours better," said Patty. Patty was taking things out of Nettie's drawer, unfolding them, refolding them, laying them gently back in the drawer again.

"My what?"

"Your family. She liked your family better."

"Better than what?"

"Better than ours."

Clara laughed before she caught Patty's pained glance.

"But your parents *never* yell!"

"Nettie liked yelling," Patty said simply, "and hugging, and Little Kids, and bare feet, and big globs of oatmeal. After Oggie's farm, she never stopped talking about it."

Clara didn't know if she was really dizzy or just so confused that she was off balance. She sat in the twins' armchair as if falling into it. She stared at her friend's drawing, at her own face—it was clearly her, really Clara, even though she never saw herself like that in the mirror. This was how Nettie saw her: beautiful, lucky.

"Can I keep it?" she asked again. Sensing Patty's reluctance, she added, "Please?"

Patty took a deep breath and let it out as she closed the bureau drawer. "Sure," she said. "I think it was meant for you."

Clara tacked Nettie's drawing onto the bulletin board in her room at home. Every day, at least once, Jubie wanted to be picked up to look at it more closely. "When's Nettie coming back?" she asked.

"That girl's a real artist, that's for sure," Mom said. Clara wanted to hug her for not saying "was."

When the big painted radiator under the bulletin board heated up each morning, Clara would roll over in bed and think about getting up. Nettie's drawing would lift gently in the rising heat, settle down again, float upward again. Watching it, Clara began to realize that she'd been missing the Little Kids and their eager enjoyment of her attention. She'd been missing being at home.

Patty still wanted to go to her own house every afternoon, so now, on some days, she and Clara paused at the corner with the elbow-crack in the sidewalk and said good-bye. They still had many afternoons together, but Clara spent time with other friends, too—she went to Sue's house, invited Linda to sleep over. Sometimes when she felt embarrassed—by her own gawkiness, by the mess in the hall, by Dad's complaining anger—Clara would remind herself of Nettie's drawing. *Beautiful, lucky.*

Clara's twelfth birthday was on the twelfth of March. She had a little party on a rainy, blowy afternoon that made the big dining room seem cozy. She couldn't remember the last time she'd had a bunch of friends at her house. Even Patty looked strange here. Had they always gone to the Knapps'? Clara remembered Nettie being here a lot. Had it always been Nettie who'd suggested it? Had Nettie always wanted to come here as much as Clara had wanted to go to the Knapps'?

Besides her own gift, Patty had brought a soft, round present from Mrs. Knapp. It was a ball of red yarn, but just under the surface, something glittered mysteriously.

"Like a surprise ball," Patty explained. "You find things as you knit."

The surprise balls at the five-and-ten were made with strips of colored crepe paper. Clara loved them, but the prizes were really silly: tinfoil coins, rings that were usually broken already. A surprise ball from Mrs. Knapp would be fancier. Clara tried to imagine Mrs. Knapp collecting the little treasures, winding and winding them into the yarn, just for Clara's birthday.

"Tell her thanks," she said to Patty. "Tell her I really like it."

That night, Clara looked at the flowered card that had been on Mrs. Knapp's package.

"To Clara," it said. "With lots of love and thanks, Priscilla Knapp."

Love? And *thanks*? What for? And *Priscilla* Knapp? Mom would never write a little note like that. She'd just hand you the present and give you a hug. Had Clara just gotten a hug from Mrs. Knapp?

Clara rummaged in her homework desk and found the package of pretty cards that Oggie had given her for Christmas. She wrote Mrs. Knapp a thank-you note:

> *Dear Mrs. Knapp,*
>   *Thank you very much for the beautiful surprise*
> *ball. I'll knit a scarf with it. Maybe I'll knit one for*
> *Nettie. I know she's very sick, but she's coming back.*
>   *Love,*
>   *Clara Nelson*

Clara mailed the note on her way to school the next day, but she didn't know for sure if Mrs. Knapp got it.

Then, a day or two later, Patty was looking for a special jade pin to wear on Saint Patrick's Day. When she wandered into her parents' room, Clara followed. There on Mrs. Knapp's bureau was the thank-you note, propped up near the mirror like something important.

Mrs. Knapp looked the same as always: gentle, tired.

Until that next Friday.

When Patty and Clara came in the back door, Mrs. Knapp was standing in the kitchen, smiling.

"Nettie opened her eyes today. She squeezed the doctor's finger when he told her to."

Clara couldn't help herself. She gave Mrs. Knapp a big hug, even though Mrs. Knapp was still wiping her hands on her apron, so her arms got in the way. Then Clara hugged Patty and left them staring at each other with startled smiles as she ran to the phone in the hall.

"Hi, Jube, I need to talk to Mom—quick, okay?"

"Raz, you know what? I can—"

"Tell me later, Jubie, okay? *Please* get Mom, okay?"

"But I really can! I can jump all the way—"

"Jubie! Get Mom!" Jubie started to cry, and the receiver clunked and crackled.

"Hello?" came Mom's voice.

Now Clara started to cry.

"Hello? Who's this?"

"It's me, Mom," Clara managed to splutter. "Nettie . . . Nettie's . . ."

"I know, Raz. Priscilla called me." And now Mom was crying, too, but she went on. "We were all so afraid this day would never come."

"I'll be home for supper, Mom."

"Okay, honey." Then Mom laughed. "Jubie will still be pouting."

"Bye, Mom."

"Bye, honey. Great news. But Clara?"

"What?"

"Never mind, honey. Have a good afternoon. You and Patty celebrate."

It wasn't exactly a celebration. Patty seemed, if anything, a little more quiet, and sometimes Clara felt Patty was watching her closely. Whenever Clara glanced up, Patty looked away, but Clara still caught a glimpse of something pleading in those huge, brown, Nettie-like eyes.

Part IV

SPRING 1959
Newingham

Eleven

Now that there was progress, the Knapps told Patty everything. The flow of news reversed direction: Patty told Clara; Clara told Mom. In fact, Clara told Oggie when she called, and Clara even told Miss Ziff: Nettie ate some crushed ice. Nettie recognized Mrs. Knapp. Nettie blinked to say yes. Nettie sat up. Nettie said "Mama," then "Papa," then "Patty." It reminded Clara of when Jubie was a baby, amd Mom got all excited about every new word and every new accomplishment.

"Papa was laughing at dinner last night," Patty told Clara one day in early April. The sun was warm, and they were walking the edges of the playground to be alone. Clara could almost hear Mr. Knapp's wonderful, booming laugh. She could see him at the head of the table telling stories, throwing his head back with laughter, then smiling with sparkling satisfaction as everyone else laughed, too. But it hadn't been that way for a long time.

"He said one of the nurses came into Nettie's room all flustered," Patty went on. "Nettie'd been saying the same nonsense word all day. The nurse said it seemed real important—Nettie seemed to want something really badly—but it didn't make any sense."

Patty was trying to tell the story the way her father had—saving the best for last. Clara listened patiently, swinging her spring jacket in circles at her side.

"Papa said the nurse kind of blushed, like she might be saying something embarrassing. Then she asked, 'Does the word *Raz* mean anything to you? Your daughter seems to want Raz or something.' " Clara knew this was where the booming laughter had erupted at the Knapps' dinner table. But Clara didn't laugh. Her insides were leaping with solemn joy. Nettie wanted Raz.

"Why can't kids visit?" Clara complained, as if Patty could explain hospital rules.

"We don't have to."

Clara turned to walk backwards and face Patty. Patty looked down awkwardly. "Nettie's coming home," she said.

Clara let out a whoop and threw her jacket into the air. Patty looked up and smiled, but she had a pleading expression, as if she wanted something from Clara. Clara wondered what that might be, but all she could think of was Nettie—Nettie coming *home*!

*　　*　　*

And Nettie did come home—the very next Saturday. Clara was invited over on Sunday afternoon.

Mom gave Clara a ride, and tried to remind her what to expect: Nettie was still very weak. Nettie still couldn't talk much, or walk by herself. The breathing tube had been removed long ago, of course, but they'd had to make the shunt permanent. Under her skin, Nettie would always have a tube from her brain to her heart.

And Nettie would have scars.

As Mom talked, Clara felt more and more annoyed. Why was Mom trying to spoil her excitement?

Then Mom fell silent. She reached over and patted Clara's knee. "I'm sorry, Raz," she said gently, "but I just want you to be prepared—she'll be very different."

"I know," Clara said impatiently, "but she'll still be Nettie!"

Nettie was sleeping when Clara got to the Knapps', so they all stayed downstairs. When Mrs. Knapp brought out the rhubarb pie, she and Mr. Knapp sat right down at the kitchen table. Clara couldn't really talk to Patty. Patty didn't even look at Clara. Nobody seemed as happy as Clara expected.

At last when Mrs. Knapp went upstairs to check, she found Nettie awake. She let Patty take Clara up to the twins' room. Clara could see from the hallway that Nettie's bed had been replaced by a high, metal hospital bed, cranked up now to sitting position. But she had to go into the room and around the foot of the bed before she could really see Nettie: two huge brown eyes lost in a white face and a sea of white pillows.

Clara's stomach tightened painfully. Was this Nettie?

Nettie had no hair—just a soft shadow of brown velvet. Clara silently scolded herself for forgetting to expect that. There was a long, diagonal scar on the left side of Nettie's neck, and a round scar in the middle of her throat. They still looked pink and sore.

Clara wished she could run out of the room, come back, and find the room she'd imagined—Nettie's room, full of Nettie's laughter and strength. But she just stood at the foot of the bed and struggled to smile.

"Hi," she said.

Nettie's eyes blinked in obvious greeting.

"Hi," Clara said again. She felt shy. She took a deep breath and went to sit in the chair that was between Nettie's bed and Patty's. "It's Clara. Remember?"

The brown eyes blinked madly, and Nettie seemed to be trying to smile, but her jaw hung loose and sideways.

"Raz," she said indistinctly, and Clara felt a leap of joy. She smiled broadly at Nettie.

"I'm glad you're home. I missed you."

Nettie just stared back deeply, and Clara didn't know what else to say. The joy evaporated, and she felt scared again, lost. She folded her hands awkwardly in her lap and missed her knitting.

"Want to get up?" Patty asked her sister.

Nettie seemed to hear the question a second later. She turned her head carefully on the pillow, as if it were traveling miles across that white sea. She focused at last on Patty, who still stood at the foot of the bed.

"Up?" Patty repeated. Nettie blinked.

"Clara can help us," Patty said, and took control.

Slowly, they guided Nettie's legs over the side of the bed. Slowly, they helped her stand. Nettie seemed as frail and fragile as a bird. Patty already seemed to know how to tap Nettie's foot with her foot to remind Nettie to take the next step. Clara remembered when she had first tried to walk after only one month in bed. Her feet had felt like floaty clouds that refused to touch the floor, then like leaden weights that refused to be lifted.

Clara could smell Mrs. Knapp's fancy rose soap on Nettie's pale skin, but underneath she also recognized the sad, musty smell of the hospital.

It took ages just to cross the room, and when they finally settled Nettie into the armchair, her head and shoulders sagged so uncomfortably that Patty wanted to help her right back to bed.

Already, Clara could feel the change in Patty. Patty was no longer lost. Patty had things to do. She straightened Nettie's pillows. She cranked the hospital bed up or down to just the right position. She guided Nettie's arms into Mrs. Knapp's lacy bed jacket and tied the blue satin ribbons under Nettie's drooping chin. She helped Nettie to the bathroom and slowly back again. She held a glass of water to Nettie's chin and placed the end of the straw between her slack lips. "Drink," she'd instruct gently, and Nettie would drink.

Now, again, Clara spent every afternoon at the Knapps'. She brought her knitting, but often sat by Nettie's bed too stunned to knit. She was grateful when Patty or Mrs. Knapp gave her something to do. Patty would reach across the bed. "Could you hand me that dirty glass, please, Clara?" Mrs. Knapp would appear with a tray. "Clara, honey, I've made Nettie some nice warm custard. Would you feed it to her? She'd like that, I'm sure."

As Mrs. Knapp cranked the hospital bed to sitting again, Clara settled the tray on the covers over Nettie's legs. The custard smelled sweet and sickly. By now, Nettie didn't need reminders to open her mouth. Instead, as she swallowed each smooth bit of custard, she opened her mouth right away, waiting for more to reach her. Clara tried to have the next spoonful ready, so that Nettie wouldn't be left there, mouth hanging open, helpless, like a baby bird. But then Nettie seemed to rush. The scar on her throat jumped wildly as she swallowed mouthful after mouthful without pausing. Clara slowed down, for fear Nettie would choke. Jubie used to choke on baby-food peaches when Clara fed her in her high chair. Jubie *still* ate her favorite things too fast, as if they'd be snatched away before she finished. Clara smiled at the thought.

"Jubie's always asking about you," she said to Nettie. "Remember Jubie?"

Nettie blinked and blinked, so Clara went on.

"Remember Robby and Donny? They all say hello."

Nettie blinked again and tried to smile. Custard dribbled out of the corner of her mouth, and Clara reached to catch it with the side of the spoon. She was about to feed it to Nettie again, as she'd always done with Jubie, but Nettie turned her head a little and kept her lips closed. She looked at Clara and seemed to concentrate hard.

"Little Kids," she said, and her smile was so proud, Clara hardly noticed the droop.

"Yeah!" said Clara. "But you wouldn't believe how big they're getting! Robby even took the training wheels off his bike the other day." Clara was idly stirring the last bit of custard. "And you should see Jubie these days. She still calls herself 'Miss Dress' when she's getting huffy. And then she gets even huffier when we laugh." And Clara laughed.

The sound seemed to be swallowed by Nettie's silence. Clara looked up. Nettie was looking straight at her, confused, but also eager. Maybe she hadn't understood all those words, Clara thought, but she had understood the laughter.

Suddenly, Clara had thousands of stories to tell. About her family, about school. "Tim York got glasses. Sort of like mine. Now kids tease us about being twins. Really dumb. Tim York's got dark, curly hair. Remember?"

Clara talked and talked to Nettie. "Remember Oggie—my grandmother?" Clara told Nettie about the February storm that had isolated Oggie at the farm. When the phone had finally worked again, Oggie had only laughed at Mom's worry. "Well, I'm a little sick of canned beets," she'd said, "but other than that, I'm just fine." Clara laughed again now at the story.

Patty had come in to take away the custard tray. "The doctor says she *can't* remember," she reminded Clara.

"Not yet," Clara said.

"Want to go to the bathroom?" Patty asked Nettie.

"Not yet," Nettie said, like a delayed echo. Clara grinned at Patty.

Clara felt hopeful at last. She would *make* Nettie remember. She would *make* Nettie understand. Being "helpful" like Patty had just made Clara feel more helpless. She didn't want to treat Nettie like an invalid. She wanted to bring Nettie back.

"Remember Miss Ziff?" she asked when Patty had gone. "You were right. She's actually pretty nice. It's weird. Even Tim York kind of likes her, I think. She asks me about you all the time. Acts like you were her star pupil or something." Clara laughed a little. "You used to make her so mad! Remember staying after all those times? Before you got sick?"

"Clara," Mrs. Knapp interrupted. She came through the door and went to crank Nettie's bed down. "That's enough, Clara," she said firmly. Then she added more gently, "I know you mean well, dear, but Nettie's very tired."

Clara understood that she had been dismissed. She grabbed the knitting in her lap and stood up. She glanced at Nettie, half expecting a giggle and a mischievous wink, but Nettie was staring blankly. Clara took a deep breath to calm down.

"Bye, Nettie," she said. "See you later, okay?"

Nettie blinked.

Mrs. Knapp came between the beds to arrange Nettie's pillows, so Clara had to shuffle sideways around her.

She's not that tired, she wanted to say. *She's not some little baby! She's Nettie!*

Clara moved slowly, annoyed at Mrs. Knapp, and annoyed at herself for not daring to speak up.

By the time she reached the doorway, she was even annoyed at Nettie. Nettie had sided with Mrs, Knapp by dropping off immediately to sleep.

Twelve

C lara had a plan.

    She explained it to Patty, then added, "Promise not to tell your mother?"

Mrs. Knapp was excited, of course, about all the progress Nettie was making. The doctors had said there might be sudden spurts, as if Nettie were remembering things instead of relearning them. Sometimes, now, Nettie blurted out whole sentences, or suddenly said the name of someone forgotten—a cousin, or her fifth-grade teacher. One afternoon recently, Nettie'd been asleep when Patty and Clara got home, so they'd sat restless in the kitchen, as Mrs. Knapp hovered. Suddenly they'd all three looked up startled: They'd heard the toilet flush upstairs. Nettie must have managed on her own. Without a word, they'd rushed up to the twins' room. Nettie was just climbing back into bed, and looked bewildered by their sudden flurry of congratulations.

That same day, Mrs. Knapp had served Nettie pie instead of custard, and proudly showed Clara how to guide the spoon in Nettie's hand as Nettie fed herself.

It was Nettie's hands that had given Clara her idea, but somehow she knew Mrs. Knapp would not approve. Whenever Clara brought up how Nettie used to be, Mrs. Knapp interrupted, or said Nettie was tired, or sent Clara downstairs on some little errand.

"I want to surprise your Mama," Clara said to Patty, hoping a half-truth wasn't a lie.

"She thinks you're pushing too hard," Patty said, "expecting too much."

"Well, I'm not," Clara said flatly. "You'll see."

Patty fiddled with the end of her braid, and Clara felt guilty for being so abrupt. "Come on," she coaxed. "You don't have to help—just don't tell yet, okay?"

Alone with Nettie, Clara pulled out the pencil and the spiral notebook she'd stashed in her knitting bag.

"Look!" she said. "Remember these?"

"Pencil," Nettie said, like a dutiful pupil. "Paper."

"Here. Take them!"

Nettie took the pencil in her right fist, the notebook in her left. Her left wrist seemed to buckle with the weight, and the notebook fell onto the covers. Clara opened it and smoothed it in Nettie's lap. Then, leaning awkwardly over the bed, she arranged Nettie's fingers around the pencil.

"Want to draw something?" She stood aside and grinned at Nettie.

Nettie stared back. "Draw something," she echoed, and the pencil slipped out of her hand.

Patiently, Clara positioned the pencil again, then kept her hand over Nettie's. "Want to draw a dog?" she asked. "Or maybe a person?"

"Person," Nettie said, but her hand was motionless in Clara's. As Clara began guiding the pencil in a circle, her elbow bumped Nettie in the chest, and she realized Nettie couldn't even see the paper.

"Oh, sorry," she said.

Still holding her hand over Nettie's, she straightened her arm and leaned back out of the way. She had to move her whole body to make the pencil finish its wobbly circle. She laughed. "There's the head—sort of. What comes next?"

Nettie looked at her and smiled.

"Remember?" Clara asked eagerly. "Remember how you used to draw?"

Stiff-armed and clumsy, Clara began adding shoulders to the drawing. Then she realized she'd forgotten the neck. "Oh well," she said, adding some arms. "First time won't be so great." As she tried to make comical hands, she realized she was gripping the pencil herself, crushing Nettie's loose fingers. She let go, and the pencil slapped onto the page. "Jeepers!" she said, smoothing Nettie's fingers. "Sorry! Are you okay?"

Nettie smiled at her again. "Okay, Raz."

"Here. Want to try yourself? After all, *you're* the artist!"

Clara put the pencil back in Nettie's hand and positioned it on the drawing where the body should go. Nettie's hands didn't move. "Come on, Nettie, you can do it!" Clara gave Nettie's hand a gentle push. The pencil dragged across the page and fell. Clara returned it to Nettie's hand. "Come on, Nettie. Just one try!" Nothing. "You could at least *try*, Nettie!" Clara was focusing on Nettie's hands, but she could tell Nettie wasn't even looking at the notebook. Nettie was looking at Clara. "Come on, Nettie! You have to watch what you're doing!" She heard the frustration and annoyance in her own voice and looked up.

Nettie's eyes seemed deep and worried. She was silent for a moment, as if finding her words. Then she asked, "Why, Raz?"

Clara's insides tightened so violently, she thought she was going to throw up. She ran for the bathroom. "I'll be right back," she spluttered.

She locked the bathroom door and sat on the edge of the tub, grabbing a fluffy towel and biting on it, hard, to keep from making any noise. She wasn't exactly crying. Her whole upper body just wrenched and heaved, squeezing tears out like the last drops from a wrung rag. The black-and-white tiles seemed to swim around her in crazy confusion. At last she caught her breath. She threw the towel at the wall.

"I can't do it," she said in a fierce whisper. "I *can't* bring her back. I don't even know *how* to draw!"

She stood up and looked in the mirror. Her glasses were askew, her eyes puffy, her skin splotchy. "I hate you," she whispered angrily. "You're ugly and stupid and useless!" She tore off her glasses and plunked them on the sink, then ran cold water into her hands until she could bury her face in a pool of numbness. She groped for the heap of towel on the floor, dried her face, and put her glasses back on without looking in the mirror again. Carefully, she folded the towel in thirds, lengthwise, and hung it neatly in its place.

Nettie was dozing off, but opened her eyes as Clara collected the pencil and notebook off the bed.

"I'm sorry, Nettie," Clara said without looking at her. She buried the notebook at the bottom of her knitting bag. "You look tired," she said. "I'll lower the bed for you."

"Thanks, Raz," Nettie said.

Then Clara sat down and once again took up her knitting.

By May, Nettie took strolls around the upstairs, and when Mr. Knapp got home, he carried her downstairs to be with the family. But she still tired easily, and spent most afternoons in bed. Her hair had grown into a thick, soft crown of brown waves that framed her white face on the white pillow.

Clara could feel Nettie watching her as she bent over her knitting. She had started a scarf with the red surprise ball. She looked up, and Nettie smiled brightly. Nettie's eyes seemed to search Clara's. Clara smiled back.

"Patty's getting us a snack," Clara said.

"Snack," Nettie echoed, smiling again.

"Hope it's pie," Clara said.

"Peach pie," Nettie said, and her smile became a wide grin.

Clara looked back at her knitting. She knew Nettie's eyes were still watching, but her mouth would have relaxed into that crooked droop. Clara unwound the yarn a few turns. She could see the next prize beginning to appear, and it looked like a real silver dollar.

The sheets rustled as Nettie reached out her hand.

"You want the ball?" Clara asked.

Nettie nodded slightly and blinked.

"Yes?" Clara felt funny acting like a teacher, but Nettie could really talk now if she had to. Clara loved hearing Nettie talk.

"Ball," Nettie said solemnly.

"You want it?"

Nettie's tone was almost angry. "Give me that ball," she demanded. Then she seemed to realize she'd said a whole sentence, and she smiled wide into Clara's eyes again.

Clara gave her the ball and kept on knitting. Connected to her friend by the tension along the red yarn, she could feel Nettie turning the ball and poking at the silver dollar. Then the ball rolled off the high hospital bed and unraveled along the floor.

"Oops!" Clara said as she crawled under the bed to retrieve it. Amazing. No dust even under there. Clara rewound the loose yarn and put the ball back into Nettie's hands.

"It's money," Nettie said.

"I know—that's what I think, too."

Just as Clara settled back into her chair, the ball of yarn rolled off the bed again.

"Can't you hang on?" she said as she scrambled after it. She returned it to Nettie's lap and built the covers up around it to keep it in place. "There."

Nettie leaned toward her, crushing the covers and sending the ball rolling again. Clara caught it and turned to face her friend.

This time Nettie was definitely grinning. She accepted the ball again, but then pushed it right off the bed. It rolled away across the oriental carpet and released the silver dollar, with a clink, on the floor beyond. Clara chased the yarn and scooped up the coin, turning to look at Nettie. Nettie was still grinning.

"Throw it," she said.

For just a moment, Clara thought maybe she saw it—that glint of mischief in Nettie's eyes. Like when she'd clapped the erasers and bowed in Miss Ziff's doorway. Like when she'd ducked under the linen tablecloth to lick her fancy soup plate.

"Throw it," Nettie said again. Her arms still rested limply on the bedclothes, but she opened both hands in invitation.

Clara threw the ball of yarn, and it wobbled through

the air toward Nettie, leaving a red trail that settled softly to the floor. Nettie reached for it and shoved it off the bed again. When Clara threw it back, a small, shiny shell fell onto Nettie's lap.

That's when Nettie giggled. She really and truly giggled.

Clara could not contain herself. She ran to Nettie and threw herself into an awkward hug over the side of the high bed.

"You're coming back!" she said. "You're coming back!"

Nettie giggled again and pushed Clara away. This time she lifted her arm a little to launch the yarn off the bed.

"Patty!" Clara yelled before she even got into the hallway. "Patty!" she yelled again from the top of the stairs. No one ever yelled like that in the Knapps' house. "Patty! Patty, come up here!"

Clara ran back into the bedroom and scooped up the yarn again. She and Nettie had already uncovered a miniature teakettle by the time Patty appeared in the doorway and set down a tray with three slices of peach pie, three glasses of milk (one with a straw), and three cloth napkins in their silver napkin rings.

"Peach pie, Nettie—you guessed it!" Clara said, laughing. She tossed the yarn back.

Nettie looked at Patty. "Catch," she said, and lobbed the ball toward her sister.

From Nettie to Patty to Clara to Nettie, the red ball of yarn drew a red triangle in the air that floated down onto the tangled red triangle across the floor and over Nettie's bed. Each time a glittering prize fell out, Nettie giggled. The ball got smaller and smaller. Clara wished it would never end, that the little shiny prizes would keep spilling forth, that Nettie would keep giggling. At last there was just a little wad of yarn left, and Nettie held it out over the side of the bed to let the last prize tumble out. It fell, but dangled inches above the floor. The end of the yarn was tied around a silvery ring with a purple stone.

Clara rushed to untie the ring as Patty gathered up the loose yarn into a heap on the end of the bed. Clara put the ring on Nettie's finger.

"Welcome back, Nettie," she said, giving her friend another hug.

Only when she looked across the bed toward Patty did she notice Mrs. Knapp standing silent in the doorway, leaning against the jamb. Her hands were tangled in her apron, as if she'd been brushing flour off them, and there were unwiped tears streaming down her face.

Thirteen

It was only a few days later, while Clara sat knitting the rewound red yarn, that Nettie opened her eyes from a brief doze and asked, "Where's your banjo?"

Immediately there was a clear image in Clara's mind: the faded velvet couch in the storage room, the banjo leaning against one end as if Clara had just left and would be back in a moment to sing the next verse. As always, she could not keep the next image from barging in on the first: Nettie leaning against the dome-lidded trunk, her beautiful hair gone wild around her gray face and her slumped shoulders. *I'm going to die. Or am I?*

"Sing 'Amazing Grace,' " Nettie said now.

"The banjo's still upstairs. It's been there ever since. . . ."

Clara's explanation trailed off into silence. She searched Nettie's face for any understanding, but Nettie only smiled.

"Just a minute. I'll go get it," Clara said.

Nettie seemed to be dozing off again as Clara left the room to go find Patty.

Patty was doing her math homework in her father's study.

"I have to go upstairs," Clara said from the doorway. She didn't give Patty time to react. "Nettie wants me to play the banjo. Will you come with me?" She tried to sound casual, but she knew she was begging.

Patty answered by putting down her pencil and standing up to follow Clara. As they passed the twins' room again, they could see that Nettie was sound asleep. One arm was flung across the pillow, and her mouth was hanging open.

Clara opened the door to the third-floor stairs, and Patty closed it behind them. They climbed as if through a forgotten tunnel, up into the upstairs light.

The floor in the attic hallway was dull with a skim of undisturbed dust. The door to the little bathroom stood open. There were two blue knitting needles and a few strewn hairpins on the sink. The hairpins had made little wiggly rust marks on the white enamel.

Clara blinked past the dome-lidded trunk and headed straight for her banjo. She picked it up, surprised by its weight in her hand. Patty was standing at the other end of the couch. They glanced at each other as if for courage, then looked slowly around the strangely familiar room. First the walls seemed a lot closer than Clara had thought, then a lot farther away. It seemed so sunny. She'd never been up here in the late light of spring.

"Let's go down," said Patty.

"Yeah," Clara agreed, but then they both stood there, wanting, in spite of themselves, to remember.

Patty stared at her abandoned jumble of knitting and sat down absently on the couch. Clara sat down to tune the banjo. There in front of them were Nettie's drawings. The one on the makeshift table had a ring of dried brown cocoa right in the middle of it. The rest were strewn on the floor—some loose ones and a worn, sloppy spiral notebook. Patty picked them up and stacked them neatly. Clara began to pluck each string and turn each peg. Even so out of tune, the banjo's bright twang startled and pleased her. How had she gone so long without it?

Patty was looking at the drawings one by one and setting them on the table in front of Clara. There were a couple of Patty knitting, several of Clara with her banjo. Then Patty laid the notebook on the table and leafed slowly through it, going back in time from the open page. That one looked like Miss Ziff—Nettie'd probably done it in class during a spelling test. On one page, there were several drawings from different angles and in different sizes, all of an old woman in a wicker chair.

"Oggie," Clara recognized out loud. Nettie must have had this notebook at the farm last summer. Sure enough, there was curly-headed Jubie riding patient Buttercup.

And there was Nettie herself, her arm outstretched, her braid flying.

For a moment, Clara was back in that high, sunny field, laughing and laughing with Nettie. The sleeping figure in the hospital bed seemed miles away, reachable only through a dark, descending tunnel. Clara wished fiercely for some bright magic that would scatter the darkness and light Nettie's way back.

Patty turned another page in the notebook: an old woman playing cards.

"Oggie," Clara murmured unnecessarily. Then she almost shrieked. "Oggie! Patty, that's it! The farm and Oggie!" Patty just looked confused. The banjo was close enough to tuned, and as soon as Clara had explained her idea, she plunked out "Amazing Grace" as best she could, singing two whole verses right through.

Later, when she sang it for Nettie, Nettie giggled and tried to sing along. Clara's fingertips were already as sore as in her first lessons with Oggie, but she played hard and sang loud anyway. She was bursting with excitement.

Patty hadn't thought her parents would like Clara's idea very much, but she'd agreed to try to convince them. "One at a time, though," she'd advised. "We'll wait till tomorrow and ask Mama first—after school, when Nettie's sleeping."

Clara sat next to Patty at the table with the checkered cloth and looked at Mrs. Knapp standing stern and rigid at the kitchen sink. Was this the same person who'd cried in Nettie's doorway just a few days before? Mrs. Knapp turned to face them. Her hands still bristled with soap-suds.

"No," she said again. "I'm sorry, girls. That simply won't work." She turned back to the dishes.

Patty looked meekly at Clara, as if expecting sympathy—*See what I mean?* But Clara set her jaw and scowled at Patty—*You have to convince her!*

It was hopeless. Patty would never talk back to her mother. Clara held her breath to keep from being rude and talking back herself. She glared at Mrs. Knapp's back, hating those ironed apron strings tied so neatly at the waist, that smooth, graying hair pinned up with that beautiful tortoiseshell clasp. Why wouldn't she even *talk* about it? Why wouldn't Patty say *anything*?

Patty caught Clara's angry glance and looked away. She took a deep breath and spoke boldly to her mother's back: "Why not, Mama?"

"It wouldn't be fair to Clara's grandmother, and—"

"Oggie wouldn't mind!" Clara interrupted eagerly. "And besides, Patty and I would be the ones taking care of Nettie! And Mom would help—Mom *loves* Nettie!"

Mrs. Knapp stopped still, but didn't turn around. "Nettie will be staying here with me this summer, girls." There was a second of complete silence before she started washing again. "*Patty* may go with you to the farm, Clara, anytime your family welcomes her."

Mrs. Knapp's tone closed the discussion with a slam. Clara was trapped. At home when she was this angry, she got up and stomped up the stairs. Or yelled until Mom, or at least a brother or sister, was drawn into a satisfying shouting match. Here she could not even slink out of the room without being shockingly rude. She swallowed hard, feeling her anger like a huge bite of tough meat that she was trying to swallow before she'd finished chewing it. It stuck in her throat and threatened to choke her. She spoke carefully to Patty, without looking at her.

"Where'd I leave my banjo, anyway?"

Patty took the cue and got up. "We were in the living room."

As they escaped the kitchen, Clara squeezed out the last required politeness. "Thanks for the pie, Mrs. Knapp."

"Thanks, Mama," Patty added.

"You're very welcome, girls."

Clara plopped down on the living-room couch. She thought she'd explode.

Patty spoke with whispered resignation as she sat in the opposite chair: "That's what I thought she'd say."

Suddenly the focus of Clara's anger veered from that rigid back at the kitchen sink to those scared-looking eyes facing her.

"You didn't even try!" Clara protested. She had to be careful not to raise her voice. She felt like Mom's pressure cooker letting out steam, a little at a time, through that lumpy silver valve on the top. "You didn't even argue with her!" she hissed. Patty just looked more scared and bewildered, and that just made Clara madder.

"How are we *ever* going to bring Nettie back if you can't even explain to your own *mother*? Oggie's farm would bring Nettie back, and you *know* it, and you even *said* so yourself. And then you give up without even *trying!*" Clara grabbed her banjo, but her first angry chord stung her fingertips and her ears. She let the banjo fall into her lap and folded her arms across her chest.

"It's not like your house," Patty said apologetically. "I can't talk back to Mama."

"*Nettie* would have found a way," Clara said, and suddenly the valve wouldn't close again. The steam just poured out in one long, burning hiss. "If *Nettie* were here and *you* were lying up there in that dumb hospital bed, *Nettie'd* find a way to get *you* up to Oggie's. *Nettie'd* have your Mama *laughing* about it by now, and we'd already be *packing*, for cripesake."

"Don't swear so loud! Mama'll hear you!"

"Who cares!" Clara retorted, but she lowered her voice anyway. "You're scared of your own *mother!* You're scared of your own *shadow!* Nettie would have found a way to bring *you* back! Nettie would have gotten *you* to Oggie's."

"I'm not Nettie," Patty said simply. She sounded more sorry than hurt. "And anyway," she added, "if I were sick, I'd *want* to stay here with Mama." Then she looked straight at Clara, with a pleading expression that Clara recognized.

Clara took a deep breath and pushed it out again in a long sigh. She had startled herself with her own meanness—she had suddenly *hated* Patty for not being Nettie. She had *wanted* Patty to be lying up there so that Nettie could be here with Clara—the old Nettie, the *real* Nettie, Clara's best friend.

And now Clara realized she had wished this all along.

And Patty had known it. The pleading in Patty's eyes was for their own friendship.

"I'm sorry," Clara said, almost moaning. "You're my friend, too, Patty, it's just . . ." Her words stumbled.

"I know," said Patty. "I'm not Nettie."

Clara ran her fingers along the inlaid flowers on the banjo. "I want my best friend back."

"I want my sister back," Patty whispered.

Clara looked up with another sudden realization. "And I'm not Nettie, either."

"No," Patty agreed.

"The trouble is . . ." Tears pressed at the back of Clara's eyes, then burned a path down her face. "The real trouble is . . . Nettie's not Nettie either."

There was a long silence. Clara heard Mrs. Knapp go up the back stairs. Her step was steady, calm. She never scuffed upstairs in a rush the way Mom did. Clara could just see that dignified back with its ironed apron strings. The sound of each measured step stirred Clara with a little wave of returning anger. "I'm not giving up," she announced to Patty, sounding louder than she'd intended. "I'm bringing Nettie back to Oggie's no matter what your Mama says." She picked up her banjo as she rose from the couch. She slapped it into its case as roughly as she dared and flicked the latches with three loud snaps. "I'm going to *my* house. Tell Nettie I had to go home. I'll talk to *my* Mom. Maybe *she* can explain it to your Mama."

Fourteen

N o one was home when Clara got there. She was never expected until suppertime. One of the dogs was barking in the backyard, but the house was weirdly silent.

Clara stood in the kitchen for a long time, just looking. There were coffee grounds in the sink, with some dirty mugs and smudgy juice glasses. One of the Little Kids' slippers was under the table next to a dried-up curl of old spaghetti. On the table were some crayon drawings—done by one of the Little Boys, or maybe by now Jubie could draw stick figures like that. Some of the crayons had the paper peeled off, and some of the colorful peelings had ended up in the sugar bowl.

Every little detail of disorder was strangely fascinating to Clara.

"It looks lived-in," Nettie had said when she first came over and Clara apologized for the mess.

"Lived-in," Clara said aloud now, and she smiled.

She went and stood at the dining-room doorway, looking. Then she stood in the living room. Then in each of the bedrooms on the second floor. It was all familiar. It was home. Yet somehow she was seeing it—really *seeing* it—for the first time, and every trivial feature seemed important.

Laura's room was actually very neat, and on the wall there were shiny posters—of movie stars, or singers or something. Laura had always kept track of famous people like that, and there had been a time when she'd patiently instructed Clara about who was married to whom, who had just bought a big mansion. Clara could never get it all straight.

Clara climbed to the third floor, where the boys' rooms were. Teddy had a snapshot of a girl on his bureau. Did he actually have a girlfriend now? Clara smiled as she imagined Teddy on a date—they'd probably sit opposite each other in the library, reading each other's favorite books.

When had Teddy and Laura faded to shadows in Clara's life, no more real to her than those pictures on Laura's wall?

Clara went back down to the kitchen and let the dogs in. She sat on the floor and leaned against the stove as they romped around and over her in greeting. Their claws clicked and slipped on the linoleum floor, and their sweet-smelling slobber dripped on Clara's wrists as she playfully pushed them away from her face.

Clara stood up and cleaned her glasses with her blouse. She fixed herself a snack of peanut butter on bread. The dogs begged with pitiful eyes, but she stared them down. "Are you new here?"

They followed her into the front hall as she grabbed her banjo and headed up to her room. Upstairs was off-limits to the dogs, and by the time Clara looked down from the top step, they had already wandered off to their favorite sleeping places and she had already finished her peanut-butter snack.

Clara sat on her bed and changed the strings on her banjo. She tightened the head with the little screws that would stretch the skin back to the right resilience. She tuned the banjo again, and tried to remember the frailing for "This Little Light." She could hear Oggie's voice: "Thumb on the fifth string . . . brush. . . . Right!"

When she got her fumbling fingers going well enough to look away from them, she stared at Nettie's drawing as if it might come alive. She ached for summer and the farm. She ached to see Nettie outdoors again, surrounded by slobbering dogs and giggling Little Kids. But she felt calmer now. Mom would convince Mrs. Knapp, she was sure of it.

She heard the car in the driveway, then the commotion erupting downstairs. Clara could see it all just by listening: Mom would be clutching two bags of groceries and trying to push past the wagging dogs. "How did *they* get in?" Jubie apparently had a cake mix that Robby kept saying he had hoseyed to carry; Jubie was screaming and probably holding the box high above her head, as if that would keep the dogs from jumping for it and knocking her down.

"Teddy! Laura?" Mom called up the stairs. "Whoever's home, come help unload the groceries!" But then Teddy came in the front door, and Clara wasn't discovered till Laura got home ten minutes later, and stomped upstairs pouting because of some immediate argument with Mom about making the salad.

Clara smiled timidly at her older sister, but when Laura saw Clara she just turned back to yell down the stairs, "Clara's here. Why can't *she* make the dumb salad?"

"Raz?" called Jubie, and Clara was swept into the suppertime chaos.

As she cleared the last few dishes from the dining room, Clara noticed that Dad was settling in at the kitchen table with his newspaper. She felt a flash of anger. She needed Mom alone. But then Dad opened the newspaper and disappeared behind it. His absence seemed familiar and complete.

"Want some help with the dishes?" Clara asked Mom casually.

"Why such an honor? No homework tonight?"

"Only a little," Clara said, scraping some meat scraps into the nearest dog dish. She felt Mom look at her more closely.

"You want to wash or dry?"

Mom asked about school first, about Miss Ziff, and Tim York, and plans for the sixth-grade graduation. But finally the real question came: "How's Nettie doing?"

Clara poured out all the facts and feelings she'd somehow never mentioned to Mom. "She called me Raz right away, you know." "She giggles a lot, now, like she used to, except it's not the same." "Remember how happy she was at Oggie's?" "Mrs. Knapp won't even talk to us about it." Clara reheated her anger as she talked. Soon she was swiping at the dinner plates with gnarled knots of dish towel.

"Mrs. Knapp doesn't even *want* the old Nettie back! It's like she *likes* having Nettie up there in bed all the time! Nettie'd come back at Oggie's, I *know* she would! Can you explain to Mrs. Knapp, Mom? *You* could convince her."

Clara was almost out of breath. Mom didn't answer right away. She swished the dish brush on a knife. Dad's newspaper rustled as he turned a page, but then he was gone again.

Mom turned to Clara with a loving, sympathetic look that made her next question all the more unexpected: "What do you imagine Mrs. Knapp does while you and Patty are at school?"

"Bakes pies, I guess. Why?"

Mom took the plate Clara was drying and put it back in the dish drainer. She pulled the towel out of Clara's hands and dried her own hands with it. "Come sit down, Raz," she said gently.

Clara was annoyed, but she sat down obediently and faced her mother.

Mom picked up a stray spoon. "Repeat after me," she said. "Spoon."

"Spoon. Mom, come on! You're being weird!" Mom put the spoon down and picked up the saltshaker.

"Salt. Saltshaker. Try to say that, okay?"

"Salt*cellar*!" Clara said with exasperation. "They'd call it a salt*cellar*."

"And I'd call it tedious, painstaking, loving *work*, Clara." Mom was using her no-nonsense tone, but she reached out to touch Clara's knee. Clara looked at her, trying to understand.

"Oh, honey," Mom said, "I know how hard this must be for you. But no one expected Nettie to come even this far. Every word, every step she's taken has been at Priscilla Knapp's stubborn insistence. Walking lessons, talking lessons, eating lessons—that's what mean old Mrs. Knapp is doing while you're at school."

Clara took the saltshaker and twirled it on the table. Dad's newspaper rustled and was silent again.

"Then why won't she let her come to Oggie's?"

"Remember last year when your friend Sue asked you to the Cape for spring vacation?"

Clara just nodded, waiting for Mom to make sense. The saltshaker toppled and spilled some salt.

"We dragged you kicking and screaming to the farm with us."

"But Nettie *wants* to go, Mom. I'm *sure* she does."

"I'm sure she'd love it, too, Raz. And you would have loved that trip to the Cape."

Clara was getting more and more confused. She drew patterns in the spilled salt with one finger.

"I'm sorry, honey. I know I'm not explaining this very well. But Mrs. Knapp . . ." Mom's voice broke, as if she were about to cry. Clara glanced up. Mom went on. "Mrs, Knapp almost lost Nettie for good. Try to understand what that's like for a parent. We try to protect you and we try to let you go a little at a time and then— boom!—death tries to grab you right out of our hands." Mom was just plain crying now. She licked a tear from her upper lip, but she kept on talking. "Oh, Raz, you wouldn't *believe* how hard it was to let you out of our sight again!"

"*Me?*"

Mom actually laughed in the middle of crying. "You had no idea, did you? Neither did we at first. 'Routine appendix' the doctors kept saying, until that night they called and said to come right away. That was the longest night your Dad and I ever lived through."

"*Dad?*" Clara felt dizzy. Nettie, Oggie's, Mrs. Knapp, Sue, the Cape, the hospital, *Dad?* Her mind came reeling back into reality, into the real kitchen where she sat, and she looked up at the real newspaper that hid her father from sight.

"*Dad?*" she asked again, half as if she expected him to answer. His newspaper trembled slightly. He cleared his throat, but didn't speak. Suddenly Clara was furious.

How could he sit there and read the stupid paper? What was he reading about now? The president's latest dumb speech? Those stupid columns of stock prices? Some basketball game? *Anything* was more important to him than Clara.

"Dad!" she burst out angrily. Without thinking, she stood and, with one sweep of her arm, smashed the newspaper from top to bottom. Dad started to rise from his chair, then seemed to fall back into it. Everything froze for a moment. Clara stood still, already regretting her impulse and bracing to meet her father's anger. But Dad was looking back at her with a twisted, almost pathetic face.

"Clara . . ." he began. Then he glanced at Mom. His voice was thin and strange. "I told you she was tough, Ann. I told you there was no need to worry so."

The corner of his mouth twitched once and was still.

Clara didn't dare move or speak. It was like a weird dream—like those dreams that night in the hospital: Dad sitting by her bed crying and crying. Now, suddenly, she knew: Maybe he hadn't been crying, but he had been there.

Finally Mom broke the silence. She sounded sad and angry and resigned all at the same time. "You have reason to be surprised, Raz, but your father really does love you."

Clara thought maybe Dad nodded slightly before he started straightening the newspaper and trying to open it out again. Clara sat down heavily. "Did Jubie used to have a yellow dress?"

Mom gave Clara a puzzled look. "Yellow dress?"

"Never mind," Clara mumbled. "I guess that part *was* a dream."

"Speaking of Jubie," Mom said, standing up, "it's past her bedtime." She turned at the bottom of the back stairs. "I'll talk to Mrs. Knapp, Clara. I'm sure the whole summer won't work, but maybe Nettie could come for a week again—like last summer."

Mom still stood there. Clara brushed the salt into two separate piles: Last summer, now. "It's never really going to be like last summer, is it?" She wiped the spilled salt into the palm of her hand and stood up.

"No, honey, I don't think so," Mom said. She came over and gave Clara a hug that bumped Clara's glasses and almost squeezed her breath out. When Mom loosened her arms a little, Clara returned the hug, getting salt all over the back of Mom's shirt. Mom held the hug and talked over Clara's shoulder. "I think it's always going to be different, Raz. Nettie's come back; but in a hard, hard way, you've still lost something forever." Mom pulled away a little and held Clara's shoulders so that she could look at her face-to-face. "And Mrs. Knapp's not the only one having trouble letting go. One of the things I love about you, Raz, is you don't give up easily. You hang on real tight."

Clara was crying silently. Mom smiled and half wiped, half pinched Clara's cheeks.

"Want to help me get the Little Kids to bed?"

"I've gotta do my homework."

Clara followed her mother up the stairs. From the top, she glanced back just once at her father, and the split-second image stayed in her mind like a photograph. He looked so sad and small, huddled down there behind his newspaper. What was he hiding from? Why was he so scared? Clara didn't think she would ever understand, but now, for the first time, she wanted to.

She didn't do her homework right away. She sat on the bed and took up her banjo again. She hadn't played two chords before Jubie came running down the hall shouting, "Raz's banjo! Mom, that's Raz's banjo! Raz is really back!"

Jubie stopped in Clara's doorway and spread her arms to brace herself on the jambs. She had her pajama bottoms on, but not the tops yet. She cocked her head the way the dogs did when they were puzzled.

Clara patted the bedspread and Jubie ran to climb up next to her.

"Can I play? Let me play, Raz, okay?" Clara handed the banjo into her sister's lap. Jubie strummed the strings while Clara changed chords.

"Amaze and grays," Jubie shouted, and Clara laughed.

"Jubie! Come brush your teeth!" Mom called.

Jubie looked at Clara, who gestured toward the door with her chin to encourage Jubie out of the room. Jubie jumped down from the high bed. "Good-night, Raz." She stopped and turned in the doorway. "Are you back in our family now?"

Clara nodded.

"Good," Jubie chirped, and ran back down the hall-way.

Clara didn't do her homework at all that night. She'd just tell Miss Ziff the truth. Miss Ziff was quite forgiving if you were just honest—and respectful, of course. Clara played the banjo until her chord fingers felt raw and she was too tired to think.

When she went to her parents' room to kiss Mom good-night, Dad was there, too. Clara hugged Mom.

"Good night, my Claraspberry," Mom said, and she glanced at Dad.

Dad turned from his bureau to face Clara. "Good-night, Clara," he said.

Clara opened her arms and hugged him. "Good-night, Dad." He gave her a quick, clumsy squeeze.

When she got to the door, she remembered something. "Will you tell me about the war sometime? And those plane crashes?" Dad looked surprised. "The ones you told Nettie about," she added.

"Oh," Dad seemed to remember, "on those long car rides." Then he smiled at Clara. "Sure," he said. "Any-time."

Clara smiled back. "Good-night, Dad."

"Good-night, Raz," Dad said.

Part V

SUMMER 1959
Oggie's Farm

Fifteen

By mid-August, when Dad would at last bring Nettie
back to Oggie's farm, the blackberries were ripe. Instead of mowing the lawn, Clara spent that Friday afternoon picking blackberries with the Little Kids. She'd been
practicing making pastry dough from scratch, and she
wanted to bake pies with Nettie and Patty.

As dusk settled, Clara stood on the screen porch and
listened for Dad's car on the hill. She could hear the Little
Kids running around upstairs, supposedly getting ready
for bed. She pressed her forehead against the screen and
watched the mist on the pond reach like a wispy hand
toward the flitting bats.

Teddy was at his job, washing dishes at a restaurant.

Laura was sitting outside on the unmown grass, reading, for the millionth time, today's letter from her very first boyfriend. She had even read the letter aloud and in secret to Clara. They had whispered together about what to write back.

Watching her sister get up to go inside, Clara wondered if even she, Clara Sperry Nelson, might have a boyfriend by the end of seventh grade. It was hard to imagine. But so much could change so fast. Last year when the first blackberries were ripe, she hadn't even met Nettie Knapp.

"Play something," Oggie coaxed. Her wicker chair crackled as she tried stiffly to get more comfortable.

Clara sighed and sat down. She picked up her banjo, but only leaned on it as she took off her glasses, rubbed her eyes, and stared again toward the rising mist.

Nettie had been up and about by June, eating and walking and talking. The hospital bed was gone, and there were twin beds again in the twins' room.

Sometimes Nettie would seem to forget what she'd said a few minutes before, or she'd hurry into the kitchen to get a sponge and then stand bewildered by the checkered tablecloth, wondering why she was there. But this summer, Patty had written, Nettie had even begun to remember how to read and write. Her parents would send her to a private school in the fall.

Nettie had been in the audience at the sixth-grade graduation. She had bangs, and barrettes in her hair. Her new braces had already begun to straighten her slightly lopsided smile, and she looked pretty. Miss Ziff had made quite a fuss over her, saying Lynette Knapp had worked harder and learned more than any sixth grader that year. Nettie had giggled.

That was the problem. Nettie giggled at everything. And her giggle wasn't the same. It was empty and silly. Sometimes Clara hated this new giggle. She knew it wasn't Nettie's fault, but sometimes she wanted to shake Nettie, just *insist* that her eyes sparkle deeply again, that her hands draw again with broad, bold strokes.

Sometimes, in spite of herself, Clara let her annoyance show. She felt mean, but too impatient to care.

And even then, Nettie just giggled.

". . . hard for you," Oggie was saying now.

Clara put her glasses back on. "What?"

"That she's so different."

Clara had described the changed Nettie over and over to Oggie, but now, with Nettie actually coming, Clara was trying hard not to notice her own misgivings.

"She's still Nettie," she insisted to Oggie.

Oggie just nodded. "And still your friend."

"Yeah."

Clara bent over her banjo and began tuning the well-tuned strings. Then she looked up. "In fact it's almost like. . . ." She stopped to think. "It's weird, but now it feels like Nettie's even *more* my friend than before." She leaned forward, eager to be understood. "And Patty, too. I mean, even sometimes when I don't really *like* them that much, they're still so—I don't know—*important* or something."

Oggie smiled. "Sort of like sisters."

Clara acted horrified. "I have *enough* brothers and sisters, Oggie!"

Oggie laughed, and the wrinkles danced on her face. "I suppose so." Then, as her laughter subsided, she looked straight at Clara. "But Raz. . . ." She paused.

"What?"

"We can keep old friends and still make new ones. We have to let go of what we've lost and move on with what we've gained."

"I know," said Clara. But she realized she had felt guilty—disloyal somehow—for wishing her friend Sue could come to Oggie's farm.

Oggie looked beyond Clara toward the high field and the Slippery Rock. "I think that in the best way, Nettie and Patty *will* be your sisters—always part of you somehow, no matter what."

Suddenly Clara's throat tightened against a huge surge of sadness and anger and yearning. "Oggie . . ." she blurted.

Oggie just waited.

"I can't help it! I want Nettie back!"

Oggie spoke very gently. "And now she is back."

"But she's not Nettie!"

"Yet she still is Nettie, too."

Clara took a deep breath and let it out slowly. "And Nettie's still my friend."

"Still your friend," Oggie agreed.

"But I don't understand, Oggie!"

"Neither do I, Raz." Oggie rested her elbows on the

arms of her chair and folded her arthritic hands across her waist. "I don't think anyone does."

Clara played a chord on the banjo. The tightness in her throat relaxed, and she sang.

Oggie sang with her.

" 'Amazing grace, how sweet the sound.' "

When they'd sung every verse, they sang the first one over again.Then Clara set the banjo aside.

Oggie was beaming with satisfaction. "You're already better at that banjo than I ever was."

Clara knew this wasn't true, but she was pleased. "I *am* getting pretty good," she admitted.

"You always were," Oggie said. "But now you're beginning to know it." Then Oggie grinned. "How about one more song?"

When finally they heard an echoey clatter on the hill, then the rumble of the wooden bridge at the bottom of the driveway, Clara ran out across the overgrown lawn to meet Dad's car in the turnaround. She went to open Nettie's door, but Nettie was already getting out, looking around, breathing deeply and smiling broadly. The dogs leaped around them.

Dad chuckled. "Except for the hair, I still can't tell these two apart." Nettie giggled, and as she swallowed, the round scar on her throat jumped and settled again. Her hair had begun to cover the other scar.

"Hi, Nettie."

Nettie giggled again. "Hi, Raz."

"Hi, Clara," said Patty. She reached back into the car

and brought out one of Mrs. Knapp's familiar baskets. "Four loaves."

Mom came out from the kitchen and went to hug each of the twins.

"Looks like a damn jungle around here," Dad grumbled.

Nettie giggled.

Clara smiled. "Don't worry, Dad. I promise I'll mow it tomorrow."

Dad turned to unload the car, but he mumbled, "Okay, Raz."

"Tomorrow," Clara added, "right *after* the blackberry pies!"

The blackberry pies looked perfect, but as she took them out of the oven, Clara felt hot and irritable. She needed to cool down. Mom had said the pond was off-limits without a grown-up there. No one was sure how well Nettie would remember how to swim.

"Want to go to the swimming hole?" she asked the twins. The swimming hole was only knee-deep.

"Let's," said Patty.

Nettie giggled. Nettie had giggled when they poured the sugar over the blackberries, giggled when Jubie licked the bowl and dribbled juice on her shirt, giggled when the flour spilled or the rolling pin rolled off the table.

"Let's go up and get towels," Clara said, determined not to sound annoyed.

"And bathing suits," Patty added.

Upstairs in Clara's room, Nettie followed Patty's lead and began changing into her twin bathing suit, so Clara changed, too. They turned their backs to each other in unaccustomed modesty.

That's when Nettie noticed the drawing. Clara had brought it to the farm and taped it carefully to her closet door.

"That's you with your banjo," said Nettie. She pulled at her straps and squirmed to adjust her bathing suit. "And the Little Kids." She moved closer and peered at the figure with the long, wild braid who sat in the armchair, drawing. Clara held her breath for a moment. "And that's Patty," Nettie concluded.

"That's Nettie," Clara corrected. Then she caught herself. "You, I mean."

Nettie didn't giggle. "Oh," she said. "It's really good." She was still looking at the drawing, fascinated. "It's beautiful. Who did it?"

Patty looked alarmed. "I'll get the towels," she said, and left the room.

Clara tried to find the right words. She stepped close to Nettie and looked at the picture, too, as if having to remind herself who had drawn it. She could smell the familiar shampoo in Nettie's hair, the familiar sharp sweetness of Nettie's skin.

"My best friend drew that," Clara said finally. "My very best friend ever."

Nettie turned and looked straight at Clara, and the briefest flicker of recognition seemed to deepen her huge, brown eyes. Then it was gone.

"You drew that, Nettie," Clara said bravely. "You used to draw a lot before you got sick."

Nettie looked back at the drawing. "Mama and Papa won't talk about it. But I was different then, wasn't I?"

"Yes," said Clara.

"I don't remember," said Nettie.

"I remember," said Clara. "I remember very well."

Nettie studied the drawing as if searching for what she'd lost. Clara stood beside her, searching, too.

Nettie had changed. Forever. But Clara had changed, too. She looked at her face in the drawing. This is what Nettie had given her, this picture of herself—of Clara Sperry Nelson—as beautiful.

"I love you, Nettie," she said.

Nettie giggled.

Clara put her arm around Nettie's shoulders and gave her an awkward, sideways hug. "Come on," she said. "Let's go swimming."

During the week that followed, Clara often went alone to her room and looked again at the drawing. She would stand there, wrestling with angry sadness because Nettie was too nervous to ride on the tractor, or Nettie wouldn't even go barefoot.

Staring at her friend's drawing, Clara would calm down. ". . . let go of what we've lost," Oggie had said.

Now it was Sunday. This afternoon, Clara and the twins would pick some blackberries for Mrs. Knapp— blackberry cobbler was one of Mr. Knapp's favorites. To-night, with the blackberries carefully nestled in Mrs.

Knapp's basket, Nettie and Patty would leave for New-ingham.

Move on with what we've gained. Tomorrow, Clara suddenly decided, she would go into town with Mom. She wanted to get Nettie's drawing framed.

"Whatcha looking at?" asked Jubie, catching Clara by surprise. Jubie spread her arms across the doorway and cocked her head like a curious dog again.

"Hi, Jubes." Clara sat down on the extra cot. "What's up?"

"Dad sent me to my room."

"What for?"

Jubie shrugged. "I forget."

Clara laughed, and looked back toward the picture again.

Jubie stayed in the doorway. "She made me look pretty," she said, as if they'd already been talking about Nettie and the drawing.

Clara turned to face her little sister. "You *are* pretty, Jubes," she said fervently. "And smart, and fun, and just plain wonderful. *Anyone* can see that!"

Even Dad, she almost added. She wanted to tell Jubie: *Dad loves us. Don't let him fool you.*

But Clara knew Jubie was still too young to understand. And Clara was still too puzzled to explain.

Jubie came into the room and began fiddling with some shells on the windowsill. Clara's friend Sue had sent them from the Cape. Jubie picked up the smallest, smoothest white shell. "Why won't Nettie draw me a picture?" she asked.

155

"She doesn't know how anymore—because of being so sick."

Jubie turned the shell in her hand, thinking. She kept her back to Clara.

"Are you going to get different, too?"

Clara smiled to herself, thinking about seventh grade, about maybe even having a boyfriend, and finding a new best friend someday. Yes, she would "get different."

But then Jubie turned to her, looking worried.

"No," Clara reassured her. Clara opened her arms, and Jubie ran to climb into her lap. "I might change a little," Clara added, ruffling Jubie's dark curls. "But you're pretty much stuck with the same old Raz."

"Good," Jubie said with complete satisfaction. "Good."